*The*
# SLAUGHTER

*or,*
### The New Atalanta

## SIMON WHITECHAPEL

**THE SLAUGHTER KING**
Simon Whitechapel
ISBN 1 871592 60 7
**A BAD BLOOD** Book
*Bad Blood 1*
By courtesy of
**CREATION PRESS & HEADPRESS**
Copyright © Simon Whitechapel 1992
This edition © Bad Blood 1993
All world rights reserved.
**BAD BLOOD**
*The Creation Publishing Group*
83 Clerkenwell Road
London EC1
Tel/Fax: 071-430-9878

# *The* SLAUGHTER KING

For Graham Young

*"Anyone fancy a cup of coffee?"*

# Prologue

ALTHÆA, daughter of Thestius and Eurythemis, queen of Calydon, being
with child of Meleager her first-born son, dreamed that she brought forth
a brand burning; and upon his birth came the three Fates and
prophesied of him three things, namely these: that he should have great
strength of his hands, and good fortune in this life, and that he should
live no longer when the brand then in the fire were consumed; wherefore
his mother plucked it forth and kept it by her. And the child being a man
grown sailed with Jason after the fleece of gold, and won himself great
praise of all men living; and when the tribes of the north and west made
war upon Ætolia, he fought against their army and scattered it. But
Artemis, having at first stirred up these tribes to war against Oeneus
king of Calydon, because he had offered sacrifice to all the gods saving
her alone, but her he had forgotten to honour, was yet more wroth
because of the destruction of this army, and sent upon the land of
Calydon a wild boar which slew many and wasted all their increase, but
him none could slay, and many went against him and perished. Then
were all the chief men of Greece gathered together, and among them
Atalanta daughter of Iasius the Arcadian, a virgin; for whose sake
Artemis let slay the boar, seeing she favoured the maiden greatly; and
Meleager having despatched it gave the spoil thereof to Atalanta, as one
beyond measure enamoured of her; but the brethren of Althæa his
mother, Toxeus and Plexippus, with such others as misliked that she only
should bear off the praise whereas many had borne the labour, laid wait
for her to take away her spoil; but Meleager fought against them and
slew them: whom when Althæa their sister beheld and knew to be slain
of her son, she waxed for wrath and sorrow like as one mad, and taking
the brand whereby the measure of her son's life was meted to him, she
cast it upon a fire; and with the wasting thereof his life likewise wasted
away, that being brought back to his father's house he died in a brief
space; and his mother also endured not long after for very sorrow; and
this was his end, and the end of that hunting.

— Swinburne's synopsis of the myth of the Calydonian Boar

# One

He had a headache again. Deep down, somewhere deep down in his skull. It muttered to him as he drove.

Too much drink.

Too much TV.

Too much wanking.

The inside of the car smelt bad.

Very bad.

He had the window down and one long muscular arm, very brown and hairy, hung down over the door. The stereo thumped quietly to itself in the gloom inside the car and his hand beat time to it on the metal of the door. There were cassettes everywhere, along the dashboard, on the passenger's seat, on the floor, like flat, shiny stones on a beach.

It was too dark to read their covers except occasionally, as the car slid past a streetlamp and the car's interior was filled for a moment with thick orange light. Then the covers came to life, flashing images of machinery, teratomata, medical instruments, atrocity propaganda. The bright colours were bleached strangely in the orange light.

He turned aside from the *Gran Vía* and towards *Colón de Larreátegui*, still travelling very slowly. His hands had shifted position on the wheel, slipping lower and tightening, as though he was getting ready to drive much faster. He reached the plaza at the foot of the old *Banco de Santander* and turned around it, looking out into the shadows.

There was someone standing between the telephone kiosks on the far side of the plaza. His body was in shadow but one foot, in a dirty, dangling-laced trainer, stuck forward into the light of a streetlamp on the opposite side of the road.

He circled the plaza again and pulled into the kerb, beside the telephone kiosks. He still couldn't see the face. The foot shifted as though its owner were getting ready to walk forward.

"Is you?"

It was a male voice, quite high, and roughened with cigarette smoking. His groin suddenly felt hollow, then began to crawl with sensation.

"Am," he said. "Come into the light."

The youth stepped from between the kiosks.

He was about eighteen, thin-looking, but clean. His hair was black and quite long. He was wearing jeans and a loose T-shirt with the name of some English band with an unpronounceable name. The laces of one trainer, the one that had been in the light, were untied, but the laces of the other were tightly fastened.

He'd never seen anyone wearing shoes like that before, and wondered if it were a new fashion.

He said, "Where?"

"In your car?"

"No."

"*Vale*. There's an alley on the other side of the road."

The youth jerked his head to indicate it.

"Show me. I'll follow you in the car."

For a second the youth hesitated. Then he shrugged his shoulders and jogged forward across the road and onto the pavement on the far side. The car started up and came slowly after him. Already the youth was standing in front of the alley, a vague outline in front of the shadows there.

He parked, turned off the engine, and flicked on the interior light. He stooped to look for a cassette on the floor. It was near the rag he used to wipe his knife.

He put the cassette on the passenger seat and twisted to reach over for the mask. The lid of the box was tight and it didn't come loose until he'd lifted the box and shaken it.

He lifted the mask carefully from the box and pulled it over his head, tapping and tugging it delicately into place. He breathed deeply, filling his lungs with the dry, sweet smell of the leather, which was underscored, just faintly, with the smell of putrefaction, like a hiss of static beneath music.

He picked up the casette and opened it.

An old favourite.

*Fleshshredder*, "Footsie in the Grave".

He took out the tape and pushed it into the a slot under the chin of the mask, checked the volume control beneath the left ear, then dropped the cassette cover back onto the passenger seat, and got out of the car, stooping so that he wouldn't hit the mask on the top of the door.

As he walked towards the youth, the hiss of the tape run-in was invaded by the first drum-beats of the track, starting very softly.

He stopped in front of the youth, who muttered, unheard, *"Puta-madre. Un fetichista."*

The mask said, "Have you got any condoms?"

8

The voice was hollow, electronically amplified, flat and expressionless. "No."

"How much is a hand-job?"

"Five hundred *pesetas*. For a thousand, I will blow you, but you can't come in my mouth."

In his head, the drum beats began to tower, and the first tendrils of feedback from the guitars crept in amongst them. The heavily distorted voice of the lead singer groaned.

"OK," he said. "But quick."

He gripped the youth by his elbow and pushed him forward into the alley.

"But what do you want? A blow-job or a hand-job?"

The guitars crashed in and the first vocalist began to shriek. Half-way along the alley there was a light, a security light outside the rear entrance of some firm. The music stabbed at his ears as he walked the youth toward the light. As it got nearer, he suddenly shoved him on ahead.

"Fuck man, be careful. That hurt."

The chorus began, infra-bass voices chanting over oil-drum arpeggios. He took out the knife.

"Take off your jeans."

The youth did nothing, staring between the knife and the mask.

"Take off your fucking jeans, you fucking gitano scum."

The youth's hands scrabbled at the zipper of his jeans. The zipper came down, glittering, as though he'd pissed himself already. He tugged the jeans down. They crumpled fatly over the tops of the trainers.

"Up against the wall. No, the other way, face me."

He stared at the fear in the youth's face. This was one of the best for a long time. In the white underpants, the bulge of the half-erect penis was already sinking away.

"Fucking queer," he said. "Fucking *gitano* queer. Fucking cock-sucker. Fucking cock-sucking little *gitano* whore. Spread your legs."

Laughter and terror choked in the youth's throat.

He lunged in, the knife flashing back in his left hand.

The first blow was carefully calculated to maim but not kill, to be massively painful, but not so massive as to pass shortly into numbness: a slash delivered through the flesh of the upper right thigh, ploughing apart the dermis and epidermis, the waxy yellow subcutaneous fat and the deep fascia as it sliced through the rich red fibre bundles of the superficial muscles, the tensor fasciae latae, the rectus femoris, the iliacus, the psoas major, the pectineus and adductus longus, the gracilis,

9

cutting the wet tubery of the veins and arteries, the descending lateral circumflex, the oxygen-balas'd arteria profunda fermoris, the vena saphena longa, almost grazing the femoral surface at its deepest point.
The second blow, delivered as the youth toppled sideways, screaming, was with the knife in the right hand, shallower but longer, slashing upwards across the abdomen from the mid-left iliac, through the linea semilunaris dexter, clipping the upper left corner of the hypogastric, on through the transtubercular plane to the umbilical and the linea alba, and on, on, up through the right lumbar, almost as high as the hypochondriac.
It was the best for a long time.
Below the cut in the T-shirt, the lips of the wound curled back white and broken in the moment before the long mouth beneath them babbled and overflowed with blood.
The youth rolled over, clutching at his abdomen.
He kicked at him, dragging him onto his back, tearing at the underpants. Blood poured over his hands. He cut the elastic of the underpants and peeled them away, tossing them to one side.
They landed wetly at the base of the wall, part clinging to the wall like a wing.
He gripped the genitals, twisting them away from the abdomen as he wiped the knife roughly on the youth's left leg, cutting him again.
He lifted the knife to the groin and began to cut in swift deft arcs.
Adductor longus, rectus abdominalis, erector penis, corpus cavernosum.
He lifted the penis and scrotum clear, shaking them free of blood.
*Basta.*
He turned and ran for the car, swinging his trophy in his hand.
He had to reverse to find space to mount the pavement. The inside of his head was filled solidly with noise. His ears were beginning to ache. As he turned onto the pavement one-handed, he reached under the left ear for the volume control and span it quickly backwards and forwards, so that the track seemed to cough and grunt with triumph.
The car shuddered as he rammed it over the kerb. He braked and stared along the alley. The youth was gone from the splash of brightness around the security lamp. He switched on the headlights and the long tongues of light rolled out and licked over him.
He was scrabbling backwards about twenty metres away. Every detail was sharp in the headlights, the spastic jerking of the crippled leg, the rhythmic spurting of arterial blood from the thigh and groin, even the working muscles in the face.

He snapped the headlamps off.

With a last incredible wrench of hateful noise, *Footsie in the Grave* fell silent.

A second, two, three, as he put the car into gear, and then the speakers began to bawl the opening discords of "Ground for Complaint".

Such timing!

The car began to roll forward, slowly.

He switched the headlamps on again.

The young man scrabbled backwards at the end of two-metre long, wavering strip of glistening blood, which had taken on a rich, funereal rose in the yellow of the headlights.

Just before the car hit him, he managed to get his feet and try to dive sideways.

Inside the car, he didn't hear the impact, just felt it.

Blood fanned across the left side of the windscreen and the youth went down. The whole car shook, then began to bounce as the wheels passed over the body.

Then it was riding smoothly again.

He braked and reversed.

The back wheels bounced on the body, then the front.

He drove forward again, and the car didn't bounce so much, this third time.

*Basta. Finalmente.*

He drove onto the end of the alley and turned off onto a back street leading onto *Colón de Larreátegui*. He turned down the volume on the mask, and ejected and replaced the cassette.

*Colón de Larreátegui*, the windscreen wipers flicking lazily ahead of him over the blood-splattered windscreen.

On the tip of the left tusk, a drop of blood hung, not quite big enough to fall, glittering in the occasional light of the streetlamps; from the speakers inside the mask oozed the b-side of *Hoi Nekroi*'s suicide commemoration release, "Hard Life's Night".

11

# *Two*

"Frankly, my dear," said Saphique Weiss, "I don't" — her voice rose, brittle as dried blood around the sleeping lips of a cunnilinctrix — "give a *fuck!*"

The last word, pronounced with an odd, twisted intonation, was caught up by the speakers and muttered away for long seconds in feedback.

Saphique smiled and stepped from the stage. The lights dimmed; little crepuscular eyes on the video equipment winked shut; and the video crew began to clap enthusiastically. Even Lilith Phyfer, at the back, expressed her approval of Saphique's performance, though all that could be seen of her in a thick cloud of incense and bhang were her slender white hands, swooping together and swinging apart like albino Siamese fighting fish.

The celebration continued late into the night.

Saphique would remember very little of it.

She woke with afternoon sun, warm and dry like silk, lying on one cheek. The other was pressed into the other silk of her new Chinese carpet. A moment later the hang-over was there, dry, throbbing rhythms that ran and mixed inside her head like thousands of pieces of rusting metal and rough-edged shards of glass.

If I stand up, she thought, I'll throw up.

She lay still, waiting for the pain to lessen.

(The carpet upon which she lay was rectangular, woven of vivid silk in many colours. The representations upon it were mostly those of formalized leaves and flowers, tropically profuse, through which peeped or glared the faces of birds and tigers and monkeys; towards each corner, on an irregular patch of golden silk meant to represent sunlight, a butterfly danced into the luxuriant ocellation of whose wings Chinese characters were subtly blended: Beauty, Truth and Life; Decay, Falsehood and Death; and in the very centre of the carpet, against a circle of white silk, there was woven in black the character for "harmony" — she had fallen in such a way that one small foot, encased in an ankle boot of black leather, lay to one side of this central character, and the angles of toe and foot and ankle, resembling that sinographic element known as a hook, converted the character to that for "autumn").

She sat up.

*Ouch.*

She looked at her watch.

It was three in the afternoon.

Shit.

Slowly, very slowly, she got to her feet.

One hand clutched to the top of her head (her hair was rough and stiff with cigarette smoke), she walked to the kitchen.

When she opened the door there was a strong smell of burning.

One of the elements on the electric cooker was glowing beneath a saucepan.

*Christina*, it must have been on all night.

She turned the element off. In the bottom of the saucepan there was a thick brown-black crust. Close to, the smell was sickening. An empyreuma. Vaguely she remembered putting some milk on for herself. And for...

Second shock. She'd come home with someone last night.

What the fuck had happened to them?

She poured water into the saucepan, turning her face aside from the steam that hissed up from it, and left it to soak.

The fridge door was sticking again. She poured herself a glass of orange juice and walked back into the living room.

There was a leather jacket over one of the chairs at the table in the window alcove.

It looked like whoever she'd come home with was still here.

She walked over to the table, put her glass of orange down on the table and started going through the pockets of the jacket. She was starting to remember something about a dream she'd had, or had been having, when she woke up. Something about the jacket.

She felt something hard and smooth in the left pocket, and pulled out a tape.

*Dysmenorrhoea.*

What sort of name was that for a band?

But the dream had been something to do with the tape.

She picked up the glass of orange and sipped from it, then turned and walked over to the stereo. She squatted in front of it and switched it on. The speakers crackled. What the fuck was the volume doing so high?

She turned the volume control down and opened the cassette. The tape cover stuck for a moment. There was something sticky on it. More about the dream started to come back to her. The details were crystallizing out of the liquid pain of her hang-over, like slow prophetic crystals in the clear, shimmering depths of a witch's thrice-heated cauldron.

She pushed the tape into the stereo.

Her finger touched the PLAY button and rose to rest gently on her lips. The fingertip was cold.

Something began to churn out of the speakers. Very fast, distorted music, with guttural female vocals that swooped between shrill soprano and off-key bass. She remembered listening to the cassette the previous night. With the girl. Very loud. The girl was a fan of the band. Saphique thought the music sounded vile. But the dream was something to do with the tape.

She sat in a half-lotus on the floor before the stereo, and stared at the cover of the cassette. A vivid, air-brushed scene that called faint crawlings of nausea into the pit of her stomach.

Atop a circular, faggot-heaped platform of red stone a naked man, nailed to a driftwood cross, was burning. Surrounding the platform, and lifting pronged, apotropaic hands at the man's agony, was a circle of thirteen women, robed alternately red and white. The man's head was bowed and into the top of his tonsured skull a triangle-headed nail had been driven from which a scrap of charring paper hung; on this the words (her eyes slitted darkly to read them) "Rex Mundi" were written. His vesicating thighs (lower down, the flames had already made it impossible to be sure) were heavily coated in blood, and beneath his pubic bush (aflame, and shaved in the shape of a skull) there was no pendent member or scrotal sac.

An arm of flame, thrown up from the faggots high past the man's left side and arm (the artist had rendered with minute attention the thousand sparks of burning hair on the forearm), licked at the bases of half the letters of the group's name, which was printed across the top of the scene as though cut through the cover to flayed flesh beneath. And indeed, on the left breast of the burning man the name was flayed, and a spurt of flame from the blazing pubes reached up across the belly in exact, miniaturized imitation of the arm of flame from the faggots. Set beneath and to the right of the upper name-flaying was the name of the album in glittering pseudo-runes: "Tit for Tat".

The girl had said that the music was called "necro-industrial". *Feminist* necro-industrial. "Femnec" for short. The girl liked a band called *Termagant* too, and she said ... and then Saphique remembered, and it was as though her stomach had fallen away into a deep well opening suddenly within her body. She had dreamed of the girl too.

Of the girl and of the tape.

When the tape had finished ... the girl ... the girl ... would die.

She stabbed the choked, infra-bassing voice of the lead singer to silence, and pressed EJECT. Three-quarters run through, on side B. Three, four, five minutes of playing time left. How long of life?

She put the tape back into its cover and pushed it behind some records in a shelf underneath the stereo.

More memories started to come back. She'd picked up the girl at the party. She was Spanish. A student on exchange. The last thing she could remember was that they were going to fuck. The girl had wanted some coffee, because she felt sleepy. Very strong, with hot milk. Saphique remembered putting the milk on, then going back to the bedroom to ask whether the girl took sugar.

She'd never made it.

The girl's jacket was still here.

Therefore, the girl was still in the bedroom.

QED.

She turned around and looked at the half-open door of the bedroom. Still there. She drained the glass of orange and got up.

Her headache was starting to get better. She went back into the kitchen, put the glass into the sink and put some more milk on. Five minutes later she carried a tray with two cups of coffee in it to the bedroom.

The door wouldn't move for a moment. She carefully put her shoulder to it and pushed. Reluctantly, it swung inwards. When it was half-open she squeezed carefully through. There was just room for the tray.

The door had been difficult to open because there was a pair of jeans behind it. Black jeans. Not hers.

The curtains were drawn but it was easy enough to see. The girl was lying across the bed, half-covered by blankets, face turned away. She had a skinhead haircut. She was wearing a red shirt — and nothing else, it looked like. Her legs were bare and one slim buttock, also bare, showed beneath the edge of a blanket.

Saphique thought, *it would look better with a tattoo on it.*

Or would that be gilding the lily?

Saphique walked around the bed. The girl stirred. Her head looked like a surrealist egg, furred and vulnerable. Saphique wanted to touch it. She put the tray down on the bedside table. The head lifted up and the girl looked at her, eyes narrow.

*"Mierda."*

"No, coffee. Tastes nicer."

The girl sat up, pulling blankets around herself.

Saphique said, "Do you want one?"

The girl nodded without speaking. Saphique handed her a cup. She closed her eyes and inhaled the steam, then sipped from it.

*"Bueno. Muy bueno. Tengo una resaca atalántica, ¿sabes?"*

Saphique took her own cup and sat on the edge of the bed.

"Speak English, *por favor. No hablo mucho español."*

The girl laughed.

"English? *¿A esta hora?* At this time?"

"It's three o'clock."

"You're kidding me."

"I'm not. How's the coffee?" she asked.

*"¿El cafe?"*

"Yes."

*"Bueno."*

"And how do you feel?"

"How..?"

"How do you feel?"

"Sorry? Please repeat me."

"How do you feel?"

The girl shook her head and laughed.

"No. *Dímelo en castellano."*

"Uh, *¿cómo estás?"*

*"Muy bien, gracias."*

She smiled ironically.

*"¿Y tu?"*

*"Bien, tambien. Tan bien como tu."*

"Oh, yes. How do you fill? Yes?"

"Yes. Nearly. *Casi.* Feel. Fee—al."

"Fiyl."

"Feel."

"Fiyal."

"Feel."

And Saphique pounced forward to fit her actions to the word; and was sure almost at once that she shouldn't have, for after the initial impetus of the pounce had carried them into the middle of the bed, the girl began to struggle, with squeaks of protest that Saphique, gasping, sealed again and again into her mouth with wide kisses while her left hand worked to open the thighs and her right, trembling, tore at the cloth over the girl's left breast.

She fed meaningless syllables forward into the face between the kisses, huskily vibrato'd with desire; and her right hand, at last, broke through

16

the cloth and had smooth, bare skin beneath it. It turned knowledgeably across the curve of the breast for the nipple; the index and ring-finger, hooked, took the nipple between their second phalanges and began to pluck and tug delicately at it; at last, and suddenly, the squeaks of protest were spiking through gasps of pleasure, like sharp spars of ice overwhelmed by the rising of a boiling ocean; and then they were entirely gone, and Saphique's expert ear caught in the rhythmic moans the throb of incipient orgasm.

Fast worker she, then.

She dropped her head from the mouth and dropped it, lamia-like, to the exposed breast, replaying in her mind as her mouth fastened to the breast the half-second glimpse of its smooth curves, honey-cum-coffee coloured with the dark pink disk of the areola spiked through with the darker, tumescing finger of the mamilla. She sealed her mouth over the areola roundly, sensing through the swollen tissue of her lips the throbbing of the circulus venosus that encircled it; her tongue came forward and flicked, apex to apex, across the mamilla; the girl groaned and swore, and Saphique felt hands on the nape of her neck, half-tugging her away, half-pushing her forward; she flicked the mamilla again, and once again, and then was spiralling its radix with the apex of her tongue, clockwise and anticlockwise, first fast then slowly, imagining the tiny mouths of the galactophorus ducts opening to the pressure of her tongue.

On her neck, the divided pressure of the hands became united, pushing her face forward against the warm mammary sphere.

She brought her own hand up from the surrendered thighs and took hold of the lower curve of the breast, squeezing it and turning its bulk more fully to her mouth. So sensitized was the skin of her fingers and palm that she felt the multiple rhythms of the axillary, intercostal and internal mammary arteries dance above the urgent smithery of the heart as the vaso-congestive tissue of the breast was flooded with blood; she flicked again at the apex of the mamilla, and then turned her tongue for the papilla-indented lascivity of the areola, seeming to taste a sweet fluid commingled there of exudes from the scent and sebaceous glands; it reminded her of strawberries too warm from the sun.

The girl groaned, and she pushed her tongue forward further, dabbing and flicking at the median upper eighth of the areola with the apex while she waggled the thin line of the raphe on the slick underside across the mamilla, slowly left-right, right-left, left-right, right-left. The mamilla seemed hard as wood now, almost painful to her lingual tissues as she now began to lap and suck and blow at it, tiny wet raspberries sounding

17

around the wide, rounded rim of her lips as they worked against the breast's hot skin.

On the nape of Saphique's neck the hands tightened further and began to knead, and the girl moaned again, long, on a note that throbbed between flat A and sharp G, baroque with irregular, ecstatic pralltrillers. It was time.

Saphique bit calculatedly into the areola, the sharp inner edges of her incisors cutting easily into the blood-congested tissue. Fluid trickled into her mouth, hot and sharp with salt, and the girl shrieked and began to struggle; Saphique sealed her lips hard to the breast and sucked, working her tongue in the narrow wounds. The girl shrieked again, but there was pleasure in the note of pain, that sharpened and twisted as Saphique began to nip at the mamilla, working her incisors from radix to apex with cruel, millimetric precision.

The girl's hands loosened and were ambiguous again, tearing and thrusting at the nape of Saphique's neck; Saphique nipped harder, and the incisors had cut into the mamilla; she flicked her tongue at these new wounds, and tilted her head from side to side to work at them with her molars, gnawing and grinding the mamilla between them.

Pain burst flower-like in the cries of the girl; Saphique lifted her head for a moment and spat blood; the hands on the nape of her neck were almost wholly tugging now, trying to pull her away from the breast; she dropped her left hand from the the warm fat curve of the breast and snaked it beneath the blankets, across the swelling of the mon veneris, through the moist heat of the pubic bush to the swollen vulval tissues.

She stroked at the slick surfaces of the labia majora and nymphae, dipping index- and ring-fingers through to the opened vesica piscis of the vagina, lubricating the fingertips for the clitoral masturbation.

Above, she spat blood again, and below, lifted her hand to the clitoris, gently pressing back the prepuce and beginning the palpation of the glans with the barest tips of the lubricated fingers. Pain had consumed the pleasure in the girl's voice; now, suddenly, pleasure was gobbling at the pain, and the pralltrillers of impending orgasm had returned. With tongue and teeth Saphique resurrected the note of pain; below, her shuttling fingertips heightened the note of pleasure; vaguely, as they thrashed together on the bed, she was aware of the hot wetness of the spilled coffee.

# Three

Sleepy from the eighth and largest of that day's orgasms, Sansiega lay with her back propped up against velvet, dragonized cushions, her naked lap heavy with Saphique's tilted, sleeping head. The delicate, rose-coloured skin of her inner thighs was tickled by the fluttering warmth of Saphique's breath, and her body shook and trembled minutely with its own electric memories of pleasure. She wished to sleep, but feared that if she did, some alteration in her posture would waken Saphique, whose next cunnilinctation would probably, from an as-yet unpunished misdemeanour of Sansiega's that morning, be a painful one.

Accordingly, with infinitesimal care, she strained her left hand wide, wide, over the Chinese carpet for the remote control of the television which, craning slightly, she would be able to see almost full-on.

A fingertip brushed, brushed the thing, and she felt as though a muscle, whole sheaves of muscle, were on the point of snapping with the strain of simultaneously reaching and holding her lap still, quite still.

The fingertip brushed again, and she managed to push the thing so that one corner swung closer. This she stroked, stroked with a fingertip infinitesimally closer, wanting with increasing desperation to cough.

And finally, with a last, lap-steady jerk, she was able to take the thing between forefinger-tip and thumb, and drag it smoothly towards her. And she had strained something: in her flank, on the side opposite to that of the arm she had used, muscles ached waspishly, and stung and pricked her in time to her movements.

She took up the remote control and stared at its control panel. It was far more complicated than the ones she had used in Spain. But then her family was not very rich. So many little buttons, so many symbols. This, to start? She held the thing up, touching a button, jerking her hand at the video screen. Nothing. This one? No. This? Yes, *por fin*. At last.

The screen lit. A games show. People were laughing and a compere was grinning, his head dipped slightly, waiting for the right moment to start speaking again.

Sansiega pressed the channel change. She never understood game shows. Everyone talked too fast.

Nothing happened. She hadn't pressed the button hard enough.

Again: and she had found a sports channel, a slow motion action replay, a football whirling endlessly through the air towards a goal hung with golden mesh.

Fuck that.

Again: and Bugs Bunny, elbow-propped at the rim of his hole, carrot lifted like a Marxian cigar, was drawling into the twin mouths of an enormous shotgun.

Again: and a golden beetle teetered on the rim of a scarlet hibiscus, then flicked wide its gilded elytra and flew.

Again: and there was a burning street on the screen for an instant, littered with fallen masonry, then a news announcer, a man in a pale gold tie, his face grave.

He started to speak.

"The scandal over the police armed-response units allegedly responsible for the so-called 'death-squad' killings of homeless people in Central London claimed another high-ranking victim today. Chief Superintendant Martin Hanrahan..."

Sansiega understood little. The news was better than game shows, particularly if she had ground her way through a paper before seeing it, but it was still difficult. The more times she watched it, the better.

She pushed another button on the remote control. The video recorder clicked on and began to record. She put the control down and stared at the screen.

The newsreader stopped speaking and was replaced by film of a street scene, a crowd of reporters and cameramen outside the entrance to an underground car-park. The picture shook faintly as the cameraman was jostled by those around him. A vague white shape appeared deep in the shadows of the car-park entrance and swelled and solidified into a car, a white Mercedes. It stopped, waiting for a break in the traffic that swept by on the street.

A window was down, and the camera swung to it and zoomed in for a moment.

The driver was a woman.

White dress, blonde hair, dark glasses.

Ms A. Kirk.

*Alanna Kirk.*

It was a sign.

How could it be otherwise?

The camera slid away from the Mercedes and back to the entrance of the car-park, where another car had appeared, a black Jaguar. It turned straight into the street, the camera zooming in on a momentary glimpse of a man in the back suit, shielding his face with a newspaper.

The newsreader reappeared.

Sansiega picked up the remote control and stopped the video recorder. She closed her eyes for a moment, remembering, and then started to press out the code to program a loop into the video playback.

For once, it worked first time.

The face of the woman reappeared on the screen, swinging left-right as she watched for a break in the traffic. The camera swung, and the video rewound, began to play again.

It *was* a sign.

How could it be otherwise?

Unconsciously Sansiega began to move, shuffling her lap with frustrated longing. Between the vee of her thighs, Saphique stirred. Sansiega turned off the sound on the playback and put the control down. Gently at first, then harder, she began to pinch the back of Saphique's neck.

Muttering, Saphique awoke.

"More?" she said sleepily.

Her voice buzzed against Sansiega's skin.

"Yes. More."

Saphique kissed the warm flesh before her face, began to blow gently and nibble and pout upon it. Sansiega set down the remote control and took the nape of her lover's neck in her small hands, to guide cunning lips and tongue and teeth home upon her arousal, and shortly began to moan with duplicitous pain-pleasure, her eyes filling over and over with the three-second video loop.

# *Four*

"Sansiega?"

"What?"

"I'm off to that meeting of the video company. You remember?"

"I think, yes."

"OK, good. Now, you don't want to come with me?"

"Yes, Saphique, I want to come, but I'm tired."

"The party?"

"Yes."

"I'm sorry, honey-quim. I forgot you weren't used to it."

"It's OK. I sleep, I'll sleep, and it's OK. OK?"

"Yeah, sure. Great. Look, I don't feel like cooking tonight. Do you? No? OK, how's about me picking us up an Indian or something on the way home?"

"If you like, yes. *Me encantaría.* It would enchant me, my dear."

"You sound like an extra out of 'Gone With Wind'"

"What would you know about that? That's got acting in it."

"Bitch."

When the door had banged, Sansiega went to the window overlooking the street and stood at one end of it, lifting the net curtain to look out. Thirty seconds passed and then Saphique appeared, foreshortened by the height of Sansiega's vantage point, walking quickly across the road. As she reached her car, she looked up and waved.

Sansiega didn't wave back. You couldn't see someone at the window from the street.

Saphique unlocked the door of her car and got in. Sansiega wondered why she was taking so long to pull out and then saw. A big grey van went past and Saphique pulled out after it.

Sansiega walked over to the phone. As she reached it, it began to ring. She picked it up.

"Hello."

"Oh, hi. Is Saphique in?"

"No, I'm sorry, she's gone to a meeting. You've just missed her. A second ago."

"Shit. OK, do you know when she'll be back?"

"About two, she said. Twoish. Can I take a message?"

"No, it'll wait. Bye."

"Bye."

As soon as Sansiega heard the handset replaced at the other end she began to punch a number, saying the numbers in English to herself as she did it.

The number began to ring.

It was picked up.

Sansiega opened her mouth, ready to speak.

A woman's voice said: "Good afternoon, Metropolitan Police Headquarters, how can I help you?"

"Hello. Please, I want to speak to Ms Alanna Kirk."

"I'm sorry, that would be very difficult. Could you give some idea of what you wish to speak to her about?"

"About *El Rey*. The King, you know. I know something about him."

"Fine. We have a number of officers here who could speak to you about that. Will you hold the line while I get hold of one for you?"

"No, no. It must be Ms Kirk. I have spoken to other people before. It must be her."

There was a half-second's silence. When the woman spoke again her voice had altered subtly.

"I see. In that case, I'm afraid all I can do is take a message for Ms Kirk. Of course, I can't guarantee she'll get it. She is very busy, you understand..."

"Yes, yes, I understand. Please tell her I must speak to her. About the King. I know what he is doing. The key. Tell her, the key to him is a book."

"Very well. The key to the King is a book. Could I have your name, please?"

The irony in the voice was unmistakeable now. Sansiega imagined the woman making signs to the switchboard operator next to her, tapping her forehead, mouthing words.

*Another fucking nutter.*

She drew a breath.

"It's Sansiega."

"Could you spell that?"

She spelt it.

"And it's Sansiega..?"

"Just Sansiega."

"OK. Could I have your number?"

She gave the number.

"Thank you, Sansiega. I'll do my best to see that Ms Kirk gets your message."

*Like fuck*, Sansiega thought.

She said goodbye and put the phone down.

It was a waste of fucking time.

Perhaps if she had a copy of the book in English. That might make it easier, give it more chance of success. But that was impossible. It was only: besides that, what else was there?

# *Five*

"Philip, have you got a moment?"

"Sure. Am I hoping for too much in imagining that you're going to tell me that you've got hold of more tickets for the Twickers match?"

"No. Christ, if only. No, it's our, uh, little affair of state. It's been decided. We want him."

"Right. Right-o. I see. And?"

"Tom wants you to make the initial approach. We'd like to keep it in at least vaguely official channels for the time being. If it all blows up in our faces at some point it'll make it easier to get out from under. It's hoped. Not that anything's going down on paper. At *any* stage."

"Of course. Would tomorrow suit?"

"Wonderful. I hadn't imagined you'd be able to get things moving so quickly."

"Well, it just so happens that I'm lunching with him tomorrow. Have been since Monday. To tell the truth, I hadn't seen it as much more than girding one's gastronomic loins before the Lord Mayor's, but now, well."

"You're not saying that he's got wind of this before I've even told you?"

"Probably not. He's a stunning old stunt but I think that's a bit beyond even his powers of thaumaturgy. But you never know. Don't underestimate him."

"I didn't think I ever had. Till now. Do you think you can handle him?"

"Oh, if he wants to be handled. If not, you could probably try him with one of your juicy young graduates. M or F: I've not heard that he's particular."

"I'll assume that you're joking, but either way, it won't come to that. He'll know what's in our best interests."

"I'm sure he will."

# *Six*

Saphique kept her hookah in a sandalwood box under her bed. It gleamed cool gold as Sansiega tugged it carefully forth from the box and unlooped the mouthpiece and smoking-tube.

She plugged it in. The tobaccos — thorn-apple, mescaline, Amanita muscaria, the marijuanas, the psilocybes — were kept in another box, in hexagonal crystal vials, each containing a quarter of an average session's dose, that sat in labelled rows in velvet-lined compartments.

Of these vials Sansiega, hovering a tremble-fingered hand in concentration over their bright little plastic heads, took three. She tipped each carefully into the hookah's little mouth, and swinging open a panel in the hookah's base, adjusted the settings on the dials of a tiny control panel.

Then, closing the panel and taking the mouthpiece carefully between forefinger and thumb, she touched the on-switch (the globe clasped by the talons of the left hind paw of the long-bellied, apterous dragon that looped the belly of the hookah), waited for the first wisp of smoke, and drew slowly and deep.

The smoke was cool and light and seemed after a moment or two in her lungs to have been absorbed entirely, so that she was almost surprised to see it swirl in front of her face as she poured breath slowly from her nostrils back onto the air. She reached back to flick off her shoes, turn her legs sideways to the floor and rest her buttocks on the dense little bumps of her heels.

She drew again on the mouthpiece, and again, and again, and a note began to sound inside her head, swelling in time, it seemed, with the steady invasion of the room by coloured, flickering, semi-translucent shadows. Upon her body, the weight and texture of her clothing began to shift, and under her feet the smooth warmth of the carpet grew cool and various.

She was tipped in slow, mouthpieced instants into another world, and sat at last on the turf of a tall sea-overlooking headland.

The sky was wide with evening and dappled blue-white like the pelt of some surrealist animal; sea-scented breezes pressed and stroked at the skin of her face like paws. The sea itself, running far and blue to the horizon, called up to her invisibly from rocks far beneath her, over the yard-distant lip of the headland cliffs, and the sun, ripe and huge and golden like the pregnant belly of a goddess, was lowering itself into a bank of clouds that were stained red as though by the falling blood of soon-birth.

She wore cool white robes, incongruous'd over her left breast with the fissured ovarine cyst of a *Menarche* badge; before her on the ground was a short-stemmed chalice of bright, unmarked silver. The Goddess herself, face and naked luminous body veiled and unveiled and half-veiled and half-unveiled to the whim of the wind with her night-dark, oil-heavy hair, stood before her tall as an apple-tree or gallows. Looking up into Her face, Sansiega felt the ache of menstruation begin in the triangle of her loins.

Slowly and unself-consciously, she lifted at the hem of her robe, folding the cloth back around her waist, and swinging her knees apart. She raised her body, feeling the ache sweeten fiercely, as though the triangle were packed with hexagonal honey-cells filling to overflowing with rich, bright honey. As she reached for the chalice and lifted it to set it down on the grass between her thighs, blood began to well and spilled — a drop, two, three, four, five, lost to the flower-constellated turf before she could set the chalice in place, cold and very smooth against her skin — flowed, freely, smoothly.

The pouring stung at her and the chalice slowly filled with heavy, liquid crimson. She seemed to hear music as the blood left her body, a cold, careful music that was ticked and splashed with beauty, like a wide river of icy water that bore frozen blooms from the overwhelmed garden of a witch; and, as the chalice brimmed and she, free hand folding down the up-hitched hem of her garment, lifted its liquid weight towards the desiring hands of the Goddess, the flowers upon the surface of the river waxed live again, and its waters were foamed and splashed with joyous fish, golden and scarlet as menstrual blood and urine.

Taking the chalice, the Goddess drank.

She drank and Sansiega found herself once more upon the floor of her lover's bedroom, lifting the warm mouthpiece of the hookah towards her lips. Her loins ached and throbbed at her, but as she unfolded herself from the posture she had taken, the pain seemed to spread and weaken simultaneously, up across her belly, breasts, weakening, and after a moment was gone.

She looked around her. The air of the bedroom was faintly hazed with the smoke of the hookah. There was no harm in this; tonight, anyway, she would be sharing the bed with Saphique and afterwards they would smoke from it, lifting the mouthpiece to and from each other's lips; the hookah was hers to use as she pleased; but she emptied the hookah's little mouth of the powdered ashes of her smoking and fed the ashes into the bin in the kitchen; and then returned to the room and turned the air-conditioning on full, and leaned against the jamb of the door and watched the smoke drawn slowly from the air.

# Seven

The new Metropolitan Police Headquarters had aroused strong emotions.
For and against.
Mostly against.
It stood on the left bank of the Thames, very close to the water. A satirical television programme had once done a sketch based on the premise that this fluminal proximity was to facilitate the disposal of the bodies of too-vigorously interrogated suspects; and *Private Eye* had duly christened it the "Metro-Lubianka".
Its architecture wasn't Stalinist though.
Just fucking ugly.
On the day after Sansiega had sacrificed to the Goddess, Alanna Kirk sat behind the desk in her office on the thirty-eighth floor of the headquarters. The room was decorated in cool colours: a green carpet and soft yellow walls. On the wall opposite the desk, there was a picture of Kali, blue-skinned and protruding-tongued, trampling on the fallen body of Shiva. The desk was bare, except for a phone and a very new-looking computer workstation across whose screen numbers and names were crawling.
Alanna watched them, occasionally tapping a key to freeze the screen, then tapping the key again to release it.
The phone rang.
"Yes?"
"The *Sunday Times* reporter is here, Ms Kirk."
"OK. Any important messages?"
"No, none. Just the usual. That girl rang again."
"Who, the nutter?"
"Yes. Apparently she's come to England. She rang yesterday."
"Same story?"
"Yes."
"If she was male, I'd worry about this. Suppose she is, in a way; must take bollocks to keep this up. Tell our guest to come up."
She typed at the keyboard for a few seconds and the screenful of numbers and names cleared and was replaced by a log-on menu.
There was a knock on the door.
She got up and walked around her desk to pull the other chair out a little

into the room. As she started to walk over to the door she noticed that the picture was hanging very slightly off true.

Or was it?

She stared at it, moving her head from side to side.

"You're imagining things," she said to herself, and walked to the door. "Mr Docken, I'm very pleased to meet you."

They shook hands. Alanna motioned to the chair pulled away from her desk.

"Won't you sit down?"

They walked across the room and sat in their respective chairs.

The reporter was young, in his middle-thirties, dark-haired, thin, and with a slight strabismus.

Alanna smiled at him, thinking, *Christina, how long before I can tell you to fuck off?*

"I'm afraid I can't offer you anything to drink — as you can see, I'm having to make do with very Spartan facilities until the contents of my old office can be transferred."

"Is there some problem?"

"Oh, those rumours about bugging devices. Everything's being scanned before it's allowed in here."

"I see. It never rains."

"Not often. And of course, you've come about our other little rain-cloud."

"I have. I would have interviewed you by phone, but my editor preferred that it be a face-to-face meeting. Perhaps it had something to do with these bugging rumours."

He smiled.

"Anyway, Ms Kirk, it is OK if I record the interview, isn't it?"

He held up a small, expensive-looking hand-recorder.

"Fine," said Alanna.

"Thanks."

He pressed a button on the recorder and put it on the table half-way between them.

Alanna said, "You'll let me have a copy, of course."

He looked at her to see if she was joking.

"Of course. Now, Ms Kirk, I'll come straight to the point. How close are you to catching him?"

She shrugged.

"It's impossible to say. In a computerized system working twenty-four hours a day, some vital connexion might be made at any moment. Data are coming in all the time. I couldn't commit myself even vaguely to an answer."

"If I pressed you?"

"If you pressed me, I would give the same answer. It is impossible to say. Professionally, I don't believe in instinct. I don't allow myself to."

"But what do your instincts say?"

She shrugged again.

"They say it could be years before he is caught. He isn't like any other serial killer on record. We still know virtually nothing about him. His *m.o.* is distinctive, almost ludicrously so, but we've not been able to profile him clearly at all. He doesn't target any specific group. He seems to have a sixth sense about when and where we're going to go for him next. This latest killing in Bilbao, for example. It was totally unexpected, but only by a day or so, because we'd only just moved one of our surveillance teams from there to Marseilles. Everything pointed to another attack in southern France again."

"Which could suggest, for instance, that he has some sort of access to police information."

"We've considered the possibility, of course. We've taken — how shall I put it? — steps to test it. No evidence for it's come to light."

"What do you think of the claims of the fundamentalist groups?"

She laughed.

"That he's the Anti-Christ?"

"Yes."

"It would explain a lot."

"Aren't they putting you under a lot of pressure?"

"Who? Me personally?"

"Yes."

"OK. Yes, they're putting me under some pressure. But my beliefs aren't relevant to the investigation."

"They would say they are. Of course, you've read the articles in *The Daily Mirror*?"

"Of course. They're bullshit. If it continues, I'll sue."

"What about the proof they talk of?"

"Proof? It doesn't worry me. How can it? It doesn't exist."

"So you dismiss the idea of a conspiracy absolutely?"

"No. All I can say is that to my knowledge there is none. I can say that the only visible help being given at the moment to the King is being given by the conspiracy-mongers. It's damaging to the morale of my officers. More generally, it's obstructive. I don't believe I should be placed in the position of having to defend myself publicly against unsubstantiated accusations. The only reason I'm not sueing at this very moment is because I can't afford the time."

"What about the political pressure being placed on your department?"

"It's unhelpful, but easier to understand. In the main, it's dealt with at a higher level, so I don't find that it occupies me any more than an officer in my position would expect to be occupied by, shall we say, extra-judicial distractions."

"You are meeting a minister from the home office this week, though, aren't you?"

"What sources you have, Mr Docken. I am, yes."

"Can you comment on the likely content of the meeting?"

"You can deduce it for yourself, I think."

"You just said that political pressure is usually applied at a higher level. In that case, why are you meeting the minister rather than, say, Sir Malcolm McCabe?"

"Not my exact words, but more or less true. I won't comment on exactly why I am to meet the minister in person."

"Were you surprised by the meeting?"

"Would you expect me to be? I have had meetings at ministerial level before."

"Do you expect to be surprised by the content of the meeting?"

"I think I've answered that question."

"Would you like to comment on the possibility that the minister will inform you that you have been suspended from the hunt for the Slaughter King?"

She smiled, rather coldly.

"No, I wouldn't. I would point out however that it would be somewhat out of line with normal police procedure. I choose my words advisedly."

"So you don't anticipate being suspended from the investigation?"

"A few fundamentalist conspiracy theorists haven't reached the stage of being able to determine police policy. However rich they might be, however much backing they might have."

"Your tone seems somewhat bitter. Do you feel that there is some kind of vendetta being waged against you?"

"I'm sorry, Mr Docken, but I get the feeling we're going to be covering this ground to the point of weariness if the interview continues. I reject the charges laid against me. I am not part of a conspiracy, Satanic or otherwise, to help this man evade capture. Naturally, I resent the claims that I am. That's all I'm prepared to add."

The reporter reached out and switched off the recorder.

"Okey-doke. Thanks for the interview."

"I'm glad you enjoyed it."

He smiled.

"Not my exact words, Ms Kirk, but more or less true. I wonder, how would you feel about continuing it, informally, over, say, a drink, this evening?"

"'Continuing the interview' being a euphemism?"

He smiled again.

"I could hope so."

"Do you make a habit of asking your interviewees out?"

"No."

"I'm afraid I make it a habit to refuse."

"Habits were made to be broken."

"Rules were. Habits weren't. Mine, anyway."

# *Eight*

On the third day, when they had started to stink, he set up his record player.

He switched it on and for a minute or so stood watching it turn. When he had worked in a factory, years ago, he had sharpened a length of steel on a lathe for the centre of it.

He watched the spike turn.

It was so sharp.

He was proud of it. He had done a good job.

He switched the record player off and put a record over the spike. *Leucorrhoea*'s "Whites Album".

He went into the kitchen for the genitals.

He had put them into a glazed eathernware pot, a souvenir of San Sebastian. It was very ugly, but it amused him to keep his souvenirs in a souvenir.

He opened the lid. The smell was sharp, but still quite weak.

He closed his eyes and half-filled his lungs, disciplining himself.

He reached in and pulled them out. They were pale, moist, heavy, like something moulded in secret, deep underground, of clay.

He had never been a very religious man, but since *La Diosa* had started speaking to him, guiding him, he saw things in a different way.

He carried them through to the record player, cupped in his hands.

The Goddess, or the Devil?

He didn't know, not truly.

But it was good to doubt. Doubts were good. They meant you were sane.

He cut the power to the record player and pushed the genitals onto the spike, guiding the sharp steel point between the testicles and up through the corpus cavernosum of the penis. He was very careful not to cut himself. He was well aware of the danger in that.

When they were spiked, he spent a minute or so arranging them, tucking the loose folds of the scrotal sac in around the testicles, winding the soft decomposing length of the penis back around the spike. It was important to have the weight distributed evenly, or else when the record player was switched back on there would be an incongruous centrifugal flopping of tissues.

He hated it when that happened. As an added precaution, he pulled out

34

the foreskin and pulled it over the tip of the spike.

He stood back and looked at his work. It was like a sculpture.

*"Carne muerta."*

His hands were moist and stank with the handling of dead flesh. He wanted to lick them. His erection had started.

He put the needle on the outer rim of the record and switched the record player on. The speakers crackled. The genitals began to turn, trembling slightly. Round, round, round.

He unzipped and helped his penis out into the air. It jerked and stiffened faster at the feel of his fingers. He pushed an index finger beneath the foreskin and rubbed it in spirals on the glans, around the meatus, mixing the putrefactory fluid on the finger with the anticipatory leaking of semen.

The first track began: a long, thalassine roaring mixed with voice samples (so it was claimed) from the interrogation cells of the Chilean Secret Police, played at half-normal speed.

He started to masturbate, sucking in air through his mouth, holding it in his lungs for seconds and releasing it slowly through his noise.

He closed his eyes, storing the image of the rotating lump of flesh inside his head like an icon, opening his eyes to refresh the image. Fluid had started to leak from around the edges of the pale lump of flesh, spreading over the spinning record. The needle of the record player rode relentlessly inwards towards them.

His hand cycled rhythmically over the rigid head of his penis. His mouth was open and he panted softly. On the record the first track had ended, and the next was playing, hoarse, static-spiked explosions over a bed of cold, metallic clatterings and tinklings, like huge bubbles of red-hot steel bursting over an landscape of ice.

The needle met the edge of the spreading fluid. It skittered and the music tore apart and reknitted itself in the speakers.

He felt orgasm forming itself from the movements of his hand and slowed.

He had to time it to end when the needle hit the genitals and the record began to loop.

She often spoke to him that way.

He waited.

# Nine

She pressed the button next to the number of the flat.

One second, two, three, four.

The intercom buzzed.

"Hello?"

Her voice. Her voice. She had heard it, for the first time, ever. Her voice.

She cleared her throat.

"Ms Kirk?"

"Yes. Who am I speaking to please?"

"Ms Kirk, my name is Sansiega. You don't know me. I have tried to speak to you many times. It is about the King. The Slaughter King."

Words she didn't understand, muttered.

"Ms Kirk, I'm sorry to bother you. But this is very important. If you don't believe me, more people will die. It's very important. Will you let me in?"

Silence for a second.

"Look, I'm sorry, I can't. I have a fuck of a lot of paperwork to do. I'm very busy."

"Can I give you my phone number? You can ring me when you're not busy. Ms Kirk, please, it's very important. Please."

"Alright, give me your phone number. Wait, I'll just get a pen ... OK, fire away."

"I'm sorry?"

"Fi .. give me your phone number."

She spoke the numbers carefully into the grill.

Another silence, longer.

"What did you say your name was again?"

"Sansiega. Sansiega Lotófaga."

"Sansiega, OK, I think I will be able to see you. I'm, sorry. I'd forgotten. I will be able to see you. On Thursday. You can have dinner with me. Tell me about your ideas. Will you be able to come?"

"Yes, yes. Of course. It is very important."

"Good. Listen, can I pick you up?"

"In your car?"

"Yes."

36

"No, I'm sorry. I ... I prefer to go by myself."

"By bus?"

"Yes. OK. By bus."

"Right. Listen."

She listened to the directions. Said goodbye. Walked away from the entrance to the flats light-headed with happiness. Her heart throbbed with adoration and love of the Goddess.

# Ten

She closed the door and put her key on the hall table, at the foot of the corn-straw figurine of a Scandinavian mother-goddess.

Her foot ached.

*"Hostias."*

But somehow, she was glad of the sting. It pinned her into the world more firmly: the world of the sting, of pain, of loss, but also the world in which she had an invitation to dinner with her whom she loved, the world of Alanna Kirk.

She tugged off her boots and socks and picked up a book to take into the bathroom with her. She sat on the cool edge of the bath and spun open the cold-water tap, and held her foot underneath the cold flood.

She sighed with pleasure.

The water was like smooth, flowing ice on the hot swelling of the sting. Like a cold, liquid, soothing tongue.

Delicious.

Resting the book on one knee, she opened it but the words ran beneath her eyes like black tears on the white of the paper and after a few minutes she closed it again, and her eyes, to picture herself over and over with Alanna, at dinner. Eating. Talking. Laughing.

She didn't hear the front door open and rocked a little on the edge of the bath with surprise when she heard Saphique calling, "Hello! Sansiega! Are you home?"

She listened to the faint echoes of call die, faintly.

*"¡Aquí!"* she shouted.

Her voice huge and hollow in the bathroom.

She heard soft footsteps behind her, and a moment later felt lips on the back of her neck.

Saphique said, "What you up to?"

An arm looped around her, and Saphique was sitting beside her on the edge of the bath, facing in the opposite direction.

"A ... bee. It ... uh, bit me. You know, *el aguijón*."

"Oh, I think you mean a bee-sting. Let me see it."

Sansiega lifted her foot from the bath, and put it, dripping, onto Saphique's swung-ready-for-it knees. Saphique's hands took the ankle lightly and her head dropped over it, the fringes of her hair tickling

Sansiega's toes. The hands tightened and Sansiega felt the smooth heat of Saphique's breath pressed against the sole of her foot as Saphique bent forward further and kissed the sting-swelling.

"Does it hurt?"

"Of course."

"How'd it happen?"

Saphique leant back, twisting the foot up to the light. Sansiega fell backwards a little, arms swinging out behind her for balance.

"¡O!" she said, and laughed.

She continued: "I was feeling very happy. I walked across the park, in my bare feet. The grass was very cool, very nice. But, as you see, it was not all so nice."

The bee had injected its cocktail of toxic polysyllables — mellitin, histamine, phosphalipase, hyaluronidase — through the plantar surface into the abductor follicis, above the junction of the scaphoid and astralagus. The pale skin was heaped with the words there, erubesced; hotter, too.

"Why were you feeling so happy?"

For a moment, Sansiega hesitated.

"The sun, it was so bright. The sky, it was so blue. You know?"

"I know."

Saphique kissed the swelling again, licked at it, and nipped, once, twice, running her fingers ticklingly down each side of the foot, along the abductores follicis et minimi digiti.

The foot squirmed and jerked in her hand and she sighed and pressed her lips hard to the swelling and bit.

Sansiega screamed and kicked and Saphique's head jerked back.

Blood began to run down one side of her mouth.

Her eyes drooped sleepily with desire.

She said, "I want you to fuck me."

She tugged at the collar and waistband of her dress and it came away, folding to the floor. The tumescing pink of her nipples and labia were visible, faintly and tinted with orange, through the thin green silk of her underclothes.

She reached forward for Sansiega, teeth grinding. Sansiega caught her hands and guided them to the releases of her own dress.

Their hands tugged at one another's underclothes, palms rotating on nipples, fingers stroking and dipping on the opened vessels of their vulvas.

"Fuck me," said Saphique.

They stepped into the bath and Sansiega grappled at her lover, trying to twist her beneath her.

"No," said Saphique. "No, with your foot. Let me..."

Sansiega relaxed and Saphique's hands gripped at her body, turning and pushing her so that she was sitting against one edge of the bath, legs out in front of her. Saphique knelt in front of her, leaning over for the lubricant dispenser on the wall along one side of the bath. She cupped her hand beneath the mammiliform nozzle and pressed the release with her thumb. Lubricant streamed into the palm, thick and herb-scented.

She lifted her thighs apart and raised her pubis for the laden hand, which slapped into place moistly over the parted lips of her vulva. Groaning, she greased herself, little slurps and pops of released pressure sounding as her hand moved.

Watching her, Sansiega masturbated, strumming slowly at the erect nub of her clitoris with her right hand as her left stroked and tugged at her nipples.

Prepared, Saphique planted her knees wider and reached down for Sansiega's stung foot, straightening it forward and rubbing it slick with the remnants of the lubricant. She breathed deepily, putting her head down and shuffling forward an extra couple of centimetres. Sansiega clenched her toes together, straightening the foot forward, tightening all its muscles and tendons as Saphique pulled it at her vulva.

Sansiega felt the heat of her lover's sex on her foot. The pain of the sting was worse, pulsing regularly in the sole beneath the pleasure of her moving fingers on clitoris and nipples. She groaned, and felt the tips of her toes brush against Saphique's vagina and slide inside.

Saphique breathed deeply again, her breasts rising and falling above the rippling bars of her ribs. She put her head back.

"Straighten your leg," she commanded.

Sansiega shuffled on her buttocks to obey. She was very close to orgasm, scarcely aware of what Saphique had said. With an effort, she slowed her moving fingers and tensed her leg. Saphique's hands had slid around her foot and hooked over the ankle.

Saphique looked at her. The beautiful, oval-eyed face was sewn with concentration. Sweat trickled down the left side of her nose. Her tongue flickered at it.

"Now," Saphique said, and pulled and grunted. Sansiega giggled. Half her foot was inside the tight chamber of Saphique's vagina. The hot slickness was familiar and yet strange, for she had never felt it in this way before. She stopped masturbating to savour the feeling. Her left

40

hand stopped moving on her breasts and hung hooked by the little finger from one nipple.

Saphique was moving herself, swinging her hips to accomodate the rest of the foot.

Sweat sparkled and dripped from her body.

A wing of hair was plastered down one side of her face.

Sansiega felt the muscles of her lover's thighs working and Saphique tugged again and shrieked as the foot slid further into her vagina.

"Goddess," she said, whimpering a little. "Lift ... lift your leg. I want to stand up."

Slowly, she was able to stand. The muscles of Sansiega's left buttock were beginning to ache a little, and the stretched tendons of her upper foot, the inferior tibio-fibular and tarsal, sang stretched protest, mixing with the throb of the sting and the pleasure of her resumed masturbation. She passed her eyes up the length of her leg, forward to the space between her lover's thighs.

"Give me your hands," said Saphique. They stretched their arms towards each other, and managed, barely, to hook fingertips together. They pulled at each other and the foot slid, slowly, impossibly, extra centimetres deeper, Saphique giving little high-pitched grunts in accompaniment of each.

"Now," she said, "fuck me."

Her voice was irregular with harmonics of strain. Sansiega tugged at her lover's hands, forcing her foot hard into the tight wetness, relaxing, forcing it forward, relaxing. She felt the muscles of the vagina clench and writhe around her foot.

"I'm hurting you," she said.

"No, no, it's good," said Saphique, gasping.

The foot was gone almost as far as the ankle now. It looked absurd, vanished beneath the sharp black triangle of Saphique's pubic bush. Sweat and vaginal mucus was running down the back of Sansiega's leg, tickling. It gathered in the popliteal hollow and dripped, slowly. Sansiega heard it ping against the bath between Saphique's grunts and murmurs. She said, "¿Quieres que mueva los dedos?"

"Wha ... what?"

"My toes. Do you want me to move my toes?"

"Your ... your toes?"

"Yes."

"Ah, yes, sí, sí. Move them ... muéveles ... o ... o ... muéveles ... sí ...yo ... o ... o ... por el amor de la diosa ... uurrggh."

Afterwards: cuddling and tickling mutual clitorises against the cool marble in the centre of the bath, moist lips against Sansiega's ear.
"I have never felt anything like it."
And then, the tongue tracing the ridges and valleys of the pina: spiralling in the fossa of the anti-helix; sweeping slowly and flickeringly along the anti-helix itself; briefly dipping aside to probe the concha; stabbing at the anti-tragus; flicking round the notch of the incisura intertragica for the tragus.
Warm breath.
"Your turn?"

# *Eleven*

She wore purple. A T-shirt in a smooth, faintly glossy cloth; clean, copper-buttoned jeans; black shoes, and green socks; her hair, in a three-stranded plait; and her leather jacket.

The trip to the house had been easy — far easier than she had expected. And the lie, the lie she had told to Saphique, that too, that had been easy, far easier than she had expected.

When she had stepped from the bus and her left foot had touched the still-warm pavement, she had thought suddenly that she was going to cry, but the tears hadn't come and she'd been gradually overcome with a feeling of excitement, of nervousness, and there, waiting somewhere in her body, of desire.

She was tired, too, but set the feeling aside, so that it seemed to be around her rather than within her, hanging on the black air as she walked down the long, silent street to the brightly lit gates of the consulate.

She saw no-one else on the street, had seen very few people on any street as the bus hummed to the point she had requested. It was as though *he* were in this city, and the air were webbed with the menace of this knowledge. And he could be, couldn't he? He had killed here twice the previous year, perhaps more times than that. Perhaps he had returned, was near her now, preparing himself.

*No*, she said to herself, *he isn't here. He isn't here. He was in Bilbao last week. He has never travelled so far, so quickly. He isn't here.*

Nevertheless, as she walked the back of her head, and her spine and buttocks and the backs of her legs tingled as though somehow in the shadows of a parked car narrow eyes watched her, and the cryptic mechanisms of a damaged brain juggled possibilities, and a foot hovered above an accelerator as a hand twisted a key and groped for a knife.

But of course, nothing happened as she walked to the gates of the house. As she drew level with them she thought, *What is the time?*, and stopped for a moment to press the light on her watch. She was a little late, maybe, but didn't think it would matter. There were two men at the gate in black uniforms streaked with silver at the wrists and throat. They were very big and the way they moved made her feel afraid of them. One of them spoke to her and she answered him and they let her through.

The house was big, very big. A white building with seven stories.

Victorian. It was softly floodlit by lights dotted here and there in a big garden. In the garden there were white statues and trees and long flower-beds and a fountain, but it was very dark and she couldn't see very much.

She walked down the gravel driveway and climbed the long flight of stairs leading to the entrance. Inside the entrance, two more men waited, older but wearing the same uniform as the guards on the gate.

One of them said, "Are you Sansiega?"

She nodded.

"Ms Kirk has been asking for you. Give us your jacket. I'll take you straight through."

She took off her jacket and gave it to him. He disappeared with it through a narrow door in the wall and returned almost at once, motioning to her to follow him down the hall of the consulate. She followed his quick, broad back past portraits of middle-aged men and women and up a flight of red-carpeted stairs.

His head swung half-back over his shoulder and he said, "Ms Kirk has asked for you twice. I think she was worried you would not come. Through here, yes, but mind the palms. Could put your eyes out, and that's too soon, isn't it?"

And, brushing through the stiff green fronds of a small thicket of miniature palms, they were in the dining hall. Most of the places were already taken under the flooding light of three huge chandeliers that hung like galaxies above the warm, conversing air.

Sansiega stared, interested in faces, clothes, voices, expressions, wondering at the big, wide-mouthed vases set behind each chair, the draped shapes on an oval platform at one end of the room; then everything else grew unimportant, for she had seen Alanna Kirk for the first time in the flesh, and now, following a white-uniformed table waiter to whom she had been handed over by the guard, the tall, straight-sitting figure was nearer, nearer, second by second.

And the waiter said, "The translator, Ms Kirk", and the beautiful lonely face swung to her. She thought she hadn't been recognized, for there was surprise in it for a moment, as though the face were an altar hung with veils that had been lifted, twitched aside momentarily by some priestess beyond and were now back in place, concealing again what lay beyond them.

Sansiega took her place at the table, aware of every movement she made, longing desperately to stare her full of the face, but only glancing sideways as the cool lips, lifted faintly at their edges, said, "I thought you weren't going to come."

"Why?"

Alanna smiled and shrugged a little.

"I don't know. A feeling."

"I promised."

"Promises were made to be broken. Not like habits."

"I'm sorry?"

"It doesn't matter. Would you like some wine?"

"OK. Sure."

When the slim arm reached across in front of her (the angle it made with the bottle of wine held by the neck in the white, short-nailed hand seemed somehow of great, unreadable significance) she glanced sideways again, and seeing that the gaze of the woman was held to the task of filling the wine-glass, drew out the look as though she had laid thirsty lips to a full glass, and, sensing herself unobserved, had decided to drink, unladylike, until it were drained.

She was wearing a green dress trimmed with black silk in celtiform spirals that fluttered slightly as she moved, like dense rows of half-coquettish eyelashes.

On the heartfinger of her left hand she wore a silver ring set with a triangular gem of episcopal purple; her other fingers were bare, and also her neck, where the skin was long and white and smooth, a field for the sowing of many kisses.

Above her neck, her face, in half-profile, was nearly perfect: her nose, an unblunting blade for the virgin forests of the heart, a sail sent scudding on the foaming waves of an ocean-world of desire; her lips, the resting wings of an unknown creature of some roofless amorous empyrean, pale and unawoken: now, as she spoke, they seemed like an intricate organic clockwork, no part of the calm, ironic planes of the face.

"Say 'when'."

And the eyes! Under the narrow, ancestress-sculpted brows, they lay like worlds, grey and alive and aware.

Sansiega said, "When", and the pouring wine stopped and the hand, the arm swung sideways to set the wine-bottle down upon the table.

Sansiega thought: *I have spoken to her and she has heard me. My words have passed beyond those intricate ears, have entered that tall pale head, and have gone beyond knowing, into the dark, sun-golden, paradoxical spaces of her mind. And if I speak again, she shall hear me, and shall respond to me. What magic I command, that I have this tiny*

45

*power over the one I love!*

She said, "I am sorry that I was late."

The head turned and she was held in the cool gaze like a flower in moonlight.

"It doesn't matter. I don't feel like conversation tonight. Do you? Speak to the man sitting next to you if you like."

"I would rather speak to you."

"Yes?"

For a few seconds Sansiega said nothing, trying to analyze the tone in which the other had spoken.

She looked away, over the table, then looked back, smiling, and asked, "The hunt, do you want to talk about it now?"

"The hunt? The hunt for the King, you mean?"

"Yes."

"Yes, let's talk of the hunt. Why not? It's why you are here, isn't it?" Very faintly, the words were slurred.

Sansiega looked at her carefully and asked, "Are you drunk?"

"Drunk? No, not drunk."

"I think you are drunk."

"You? You think I'm drunk? But who are you? I've forgotten your name."

"Well, ask me. But is it polite, amongst the English, to forget the name of a guest?"

"No, I don't think so. I don't care. But I'll ask you anyway. Who are you?"

"I am Sansiega."

"Sansiega? Sansiega what? Or just Sansiega?"

"As you like."

"I think just Sansiega. It's a pretty name, don't you think?"

"How can I tell? I have it since I was very small. But it is an old-fashioned name, in these days. That's right, isn't it, 'old-fashioned?'"

"Yes, perfect, I think."

She smiled faintly, and said, "And tell me, Sansiega, do you know who I am?"

"Who you are? Of course."

"Tell me then."

"Tell you?"

"Yes."

"Well, you are Alanna Kirk. Is that a pretty name, in English?"

"How can I tell? I've had it since I was very small."

46

"I think that it is pretty."

"Perhaps you do. Here, pick up your glass. Like this, yes? OK? Right, I like your name and you like mine, so let's toast each other. You don't understand? Like this. First, to you. To Sansiega. You say, 'to me', and we clink glasses, like this."

"To me."

"Good. Now, to me. You say it."

"To you. To Alanna."

"To me."

And for the first time she laughed fully.

"And now we drink. But I don't like wine very much."

"I neither."

"You neither? Then, how similar we are!"

"Similar? But this is only a small thing."

"No, a disliking for wine is something very big. To me. Not to you?"

"To me? I don't know. I think you are lying. I think you are making a joke of me."

"No, don't accuse me of that."

And under the table, Sansiega's ankle flared sharply with pain.

"You kicked me!"

"Well, kick me back."

But she had folded her legs up on her chair. Laughing, Sansiega punched at her knees, but her fist was caught and held tight.

Alanna said, mockingly, "Your fist feels like a shell. A little shell. Just like a little shell."

"You are very strong."

"When I squeeze hard, does it hurt? Like this?"

"A little. But I like it."

Then both sensed suddenly that those sitting near them had become aware of the little games they played, had felt the tug of the currents awakened by the quick little erotic whirlpools that swirled and died at both their loins.

They sat straight on their chairs again, unsmiling.

Sansiega asked, "When will they serve? The dinner, I mean."

"Do you want to eat?"

"Yes, of course. I am hungry."

Alanna was silent for a moment, then said, "Nevertheless, when the dinner comes, say 'no' to it."

"'No'? And you, will you say 'no'?"

"Ten minutes ago, no, I would have said 'yes'. I have waited for this meal for a long time. When they asked me, I would have said, 'yes'. Yessss pleasssse. Like a snake, you know."

Sansiega laughed.

She said, "You are not a snake."

"Ah, but I am. I am a golden snake that loves the sun. Can you not picture me, lying on green moss beside a forest pool in the sun?"

"I do not understand you very well, but you are not a snake. You are a ... I don't know the word in English. In Spanish, *un halcón*. It is a sort of bird."

"An owl?"

"What is that?"

Alanna made circles of her thumbs and index fingers and lifted them to her eyes. She hooted softly three times, then lowered her hands.

Sansiega laughed again.

She said, "That is very good. You would be a good owl. But it is not 'owl' that I want to say."

"Eagle, then?"

"No, I know 'eagle'. Very big and strong, no? Fierce?"

"Yes. Well, neither eagle nor owl. But I don't want to know. At the moment, I can think you have paid me a compliment. Perhaps if I learn what you said, I won't think that. Look, dinner is about to be served. Look around the table, at the people. They are very beautiful, don't you think?"

Sansiega looked around the table. There were fifty-seven people. She counted them, under her breath, wanting to practice her English, her mind working sweetly and well with happiness. The women wore dresses of many different kinds, many different colours and Sansiega thought the rustle of bright cloth beneath the soft, hive-like hum of conversation, the occasional clear note of wine glasses kissed in joking toast, was like the breath of a dry, ghostly ocean, sighing and sighing on the dark, varnished island of the table.

The men wore black dinner-jackets and bow ties, mostly; a few were dressed more casually, in jeans and brightly-coloured T-shirts (one of them said *LOUD & QUEER* above a picture of a screaming mouth inside a pink triangle: she didn't understand it).

At each place a careful hierarchy of cutlery had been laid, knives and forks and spoons of a dozen different types in lustrous silver; and laid also at each place was a capped silver pot that sat to the table on slender, cat-footed legs.

The wine glasses were crystal, tall and slim and with rims that flared faintly, as though they were the mouths of small sweet trumpets. Sansiega imagined the note she would hear if the glasses began to sound. An odd note, unpredictable to the level of the dark, sanguineous wine in each glass (the throats of trumpets choked variously with blood).

There were napkins of plain white silk, rolled and ringed in silver, that silent servants in black were now sliding free and unfurling to lay across waiting laps.

A servant was at Alanna's right shoulder, reaching for her napkin. She touched his sleeve, very briefly, and shook her head as his face turned to hers. He stepped back and around to Sansiega but she, looking into Alanna's face and the thin lips rounded on a silent 'no', shook her head too, and their napkins remained rolled, ringed in silver.

So, they would be spectators and not participate.

Sansiega hoped the food would not be very delicious-looking, or smell too appetizing, for already her stomach felt a little empty, and if the food that she could not eat seemed very good, she feared that it would start to rumble, which Alanna would, she thought, make a joke of, and this would be all very well, but for her not very dignified.

Tall-sided trolleys were wheeled in by the servants. The trolleys rattled very faintly. The sides were run open, left and right, and white- gloved hands probed shadowed interiors to emerge with soup plates of pure white porcelain that flashed like bright rictuses as the plates were laid to the surface of the table.

Sansiega had drunk all of her wine and a servant, before she could stop him, had poured her more. She picked up the glass and sipped at the wine. Her head felt a little hollow, as though some of the light of the chandeliers had got inside and had grown there, and she knew she was beginning to be a little drunk. She turned to Alanna and whispered, "What will be the first course?"

Alanna laid a finger of her right hand across her lips and indicated an ear with a finger of her left.

Listen.

Silent now, the trolleys were wheeled out; a moment passed, and more trolleys, more slowly, were wheeled in. These carried huge tureens of low-lustred silver, whose covers were shaped like Phrygian caps, with a suggestion of flopping, rough-napped cloth marvellously rendered in the working of the silver; at the apices gleamed tiny crystal (for a moment Sansiega could not be sure what they were, then saw that they were) skulls, odd little crystal skulls that were neither human nor animal, but a hybrid of both. Wisps of steam curled up around the rims of the covers; as the covers were lifted away and each tureen was bowed upon by a servant holding a beautifully light and capacious ladle, the steam gushed up fully, heavy with the flavour and heat of the soup.

Sansiega drew her lower lip a little inside her mouth and bit down quite hard it, to distract her stomach; and as she did so, speakers awoke at secret points in the room, and a single resonant note, the note of a bell, sounded. A moment after, a rich contralto voice (it was impossible to decide whether it was low female or high male), speaking French, said, "Death Cap soup."

The soup that poured from the ladles to the plates was a clear brown in which there tiny cubes of white.

Looking from tureen to tureen, from white-gloved ladler to white-gloved ladler, Sansiega was unable to find any individuality; imperceptibly, the light of the chandeliers had been dimmed, and the room was greenly shadowed; the faces of the ladlers were expressionless, save for a slight pursing of the lips, and all movements were smooth and minimalistically skilful, so that although there was no impression of speed the fifty-five plates were swiftly filled.

Then the tureens were capped and the trolleys wheeled away, a little more quickly than they had been wheeled in.

Sansiega started to look around her, at the faces above the plates, and her eyes stumbled, returned to where they had started and started again. They circled the table once, twice and she frowned a little at what they told her, for in the faces there were strange yet related expressions, differing from guest to guest only in the proportions of the varying emotions that constituted them: strange expressions that contained both anxiety and anticipation: fear, perhaps, and wonderment, as each guest, save herself and Alanna, gazed down into their steaming circle of soup as though a great mystery were concealed there.

Then spoons were lifted and poised; a pause; the spoons dipped to the soup, were filled, were lifted to awed, opening mouths, and auto-eucharistic knots were tied and untied in fifty-five throats.

The silence was gently broken: an old man swung his head to a neighbour and spoke; the spoons dipped and rose through the slowly re-awoken hum of conversation; dipped and rose; dipped and rose; there was the clatter of a fallen spoon: a young woman had gagged on the soup and dropped her head, had half-turned in her chair, to vomit into the vase set behind her, a hand raised, palm lifted, flat and vertical in apology; servants were with her in a moment, discreetly lifting the plate and mopping at the spilled soup; the young woman sat straight, dabbing her lips with her napkin; the dropped spoon was lifted away and replaced with a clean; the young woman dropped the napkin into the hands of a servant and received a fresh, picked up her new spoon and began her soup again; a few eyes had swung to her but the incident seemed mostly unremarked; the hum of conversation was pricked through with little ringing notes as the spoons dipped into emptying plates; the eating had been swift, pursued with a half-enthusiastic reluctance, a half-reluctant enthusiasm; already, people chased the last traces of their soup, spoons to porcelain; Sansiega lifted her wine and sipped; beside her Alanna sat silently, watching; the young woman who had vomited stopped eating for a moment and stroked down her throat lightly with her fingertips, once, eyes closed; her eyes opened and she reached to tip the plate just a little towards her, waiting a second for the soup to drain deeper for her spoon, a grown crescent of brown within the white circle of the plate; the spoon curved against the crescent, capturing it, and was lifted and emptied; for a second Sansiega caught the woman's eyes; beneath them the tip of a red tongue was circling the lips minutely for traces of soup; simultaneously, they looked away from each other; no message had passed between them.

When all the guests were finished the servants moved in on the table. Each lifted and carried two plates, balancing one to a hand on up-curved fingers, and took them from the room. As the last of the carriers-out left the room the first of the carriers-in entered it bearing the single plate of the second course. There had been a subtle, minimal choreography to the thing; the plates carried in were black, with a simple white decorative ring on the inner rim, and seemed empty.

The plates were laid to the surface of the table and Sansiega saw that what she had thought a decoration, the white inner ring, was the second course: tiny, circular slices of raw fish, overlapped to a perfect circle. On the speakers the bell tolled twice and the epicene voice said, "Raw balloon fish."

Small forks were lifted by the guests and the second course begun. The forks dipped and speared the slices of fish like tiny silver beaks; the tiny slices were lifted and fed to absurd, huge mouths. There was little talking over this course, monosyllables from neighbour to neighbour, occasionally; mostly the mouths opened and closed and worked over the tiny raw slices in silence; this time the eating was slow, almost meditative, as though the flavour of the fish were something subtle, very faint, that required concentration to appreciate.

The little forks glittered, rising and falling from and to the black plates;

the rings of white ran back to crescents and were gone; one hundred and ten black, lidless eyes gazed to the chandeliers; the servants moved in on the table again and the plates were lifted and carried away.

Around the table, conversation began again, but there was a strangeness in it. As the guests talked, some pouted, flexed their lips in momentary smiles, and there seemed an exaggerated care to the articulation of the words in the conversations Sansiega could hear, as though those speaking felt their lips and tongues frozen and feared that they should mumble if they did not force energy into their speaking. To Alanna, Sansiega said, almost whispering, "It's strange, isn't it, this dinner party?"

Alanna looked at her. She said, "Strange? Do you not understand it yet?"

"No. What is there to understand? It is strange, but it is only a dinner party."

Alanna picked up her glass of wine and sipped from it. Trolleys were being wheeled into the room for the third course. She said teasingly, "Sansiegaaaaa."

"Yes?"

"Is that a beautiful name?"

"You must tell me. I do not know."

"It is a beautiful name."

On the trolleys were long oval silver dishes, domed over with highly polished covers that twisted their reflection of the room to phantasmagoria (the servants loomed and stalked on the silver like Titans; of the guests, at the table, the women were vivid and vulturine, death-goddesses presiding the judgment of the men, who sat stern and Rhadamanthine in black). Sansiega thought that she could catch, rising through the fading hum of the conversation around the table another hum, a deeper, more regular, on a single unvarying note, from beneath the covers.

A bee-note.

On the speakers the bell tolled three times.

The voice said, "Live bees with honey."

The covers were lifted back.

Onto the air of the now silent room the voices of the angry bees burst loudly: each cover had lifted back to reveal a living circle, a glossy, dancing pie of bees buzzing and jerking enraged against short threads that held them leashed to a base of pastry. The sides of the trolleys were run back and servants stooped to lift squat, heavy plate-towers up beside the bee-pies.

Silver pie-slices were taken up and laid delicately, calculatedly (the handles held almost vertically, so that bare fingers were kept clear of the dancing bees) to the centres of the pies; a moment of resistance and the beaks of the pie-slices had dropped through the pastry and were marching back, inch-inch-inch, to the edges of the pies.

Reached, the edges were deserted for the centres; the pie-dishes were rotated smoothly through ten minutes of arc; second radiuses marched from centres to edges; the pie-slices were turned flat and the triangular slices of pie levered to them, lifted, turned, laid to the surface of plates. As the plates were carried to the table Sansiega heard subtle dopplerings of the bee-notes, woven into the majority voices of the pies, that ended as the plates were set upon the table. She watched the nearest, fascinated. A sharp little triangle of bee-pie, dancing and singing in rage! She saw now how the threads were attached to the bees by a blob of cement on the underside of the thorax, how the threads were twanged and plucked on the bees' frustrated flight, how the bees' wings were silver smears of energy.

More plates were laid to the table, more dark enraged triangles of bee-pie dancing glossily against the white of the plates. The pies were eaten back, slice by slice, and then they were nothing, and the table was ringed, save for Sansiega's place and Alanna's, with the bee-triangles.

From the array of cutlery the guests chose round-bowled spoons, and reached forward to uncap the little silver pots that stood at each place. The spoons were dipped into the pots, lifted, thick with honey that was wound to the spoon-bowl and brought back to hang above the slices of pie. The honey began to flow slowly from the spoons, blunt tongues of amber and gold that licked down, longer, sharper, and all at once, a dozen times around the table, had touched the pie and flowed, coiling, across the dance of the bees.

The spoons swayed above the bee-triangles and the honey poured thinly to them, choking the bees' anger in sweet, thick gold; the notes thickened and quietened beneath the honey, the smeared silver wings slowed or paralyzed, and the bees crawled to and fro on the pastry, leashed in place like tiny drenched dogs.

Now, laying the spoons back into the honey-pots, the guests selected pie-forks and bent to their honey-smothered slices of pie, cutting out pieces with great care, lifting them to reluctant, opening, eager mouths: three, four, five melilucent bees on white pastry on silver forks, lifted to moist red mouths.

Lifted into.

The mouths closed and the low buzzing of the bees was lessened, thickened further, coming through the flesh-walls of cheeks that bunched and gathered to the working of the jaws.

Sansiega heard the dry-wet *crunch-crunch* of the bees' tiny dark deaths and sudden choked back cries of pain, which began to burn slowly in the faces around her. She watched the eyes grow round and wet and hot with the wonder of the cruelty of the stings.

One man did not chew; his mouth closed over his forkful of bee-pie and remained still; his throat knotted hugely and he had swallowed and the pain of the stings in the flesh of his inner throat must have been very great, for his mouth fell open, breathless, and a thread of saliva crept slowly down the groove of a laughter-line; a few moments after this, sweet little Lazarus from the vagina dentata of the mouth, a bee crawled over his lower lip and down his chin, unsteadily, sodden with saliva and honey, writing a glistening character into the stubble-shadowed skin; above it, the mouth fell open wider, and below it the man's hands rose and clamped on the neck, left over right: a dark, hairy hand, the left was, hiding its brother from view: its knuckles were like huge pearls, white with the strength of the hand's grip; and the eyes were opening very wide now in a face tinged with approaching suffocation.

Sansiega imagined the face suddenly to be a palette into which Death would mix single colours for the painting of thanatopses in the brain behind; she watched it darken from pink to red to crimson, to a crimson of such intensity and evenness that it became difficult to make out the features of the face beneath it, the face that had bloated and grown smooth (the bee, saliva-clung to the skin, had followed the curve of the chin downwards, to the throat and the hands, and rested now on the left forefinger, sampling its wet wings against the air); into the crimson face, now, blue began to seep, darkening it to purple, the purple of the gown of an Empress assassinated (the knives leaping and leaping like salmon against the waterfall of the body), and deeper, to a purple that passed beyond purple and became blue, the blue of very deep water (a lake, and fleet wavelets striking the shore at the foot of a grove-shadowed temple of white marble); the man began to tip sideways and the woman next to him, politely, shuffled her chair to give him room; on his neck, his head grew heavy, flopped forward on the hairy, empearled collar of the hands; the edge of the table was like a sea, rising to swallow him; he was beneath it; Sansiega felt the shake of his body in the floor beneath her feet and heard the clatter of his overfallen chair.

She looked around the table and saw that in other faces the chromatic progressions of suffocation had begun. Servants were carrying the dead man from the room, familiar with the heavy fluidity of the limbs, the lolling of the head and flaccidity of the torso. Sansiega noticed cheeks — so many! — puffing irregularly with the poison of the stings: a corner of the mouth of one girl was swollen smooth and ripe like a fruit, misshaping the twin curves of her lips; Sansiega imagined kissing them: they would be hot, would tremble and flutter beneath hers with the pain of the sting; the girl lifted the last of her bee-triangle; her mouth opened oddly and closed; she chewed and her eyes flickered on the pain of the chewing.

Sansiega took her eyes from the girl's face and looked around the table again. On many plates fragments of pie remained, dark and dancing. Behind them the guests were uneating from pain of previous eating or passed pink-red-crimson-purple-blue to death. Two more were dead, a woman and man. They were carried from the room. The servants were lifting away the plates of those unable to continue and setting glasses of iced water down instead. As the glasses were lifted to the reddened, swollen faces Sansiega heard ice-cubes tinkle delicately through the diminished buzzing of the bees. Others had finished their slices of pie and sat back to wait for the servants to take away their plates.

No-one spoke. The ice tinkled in the glasses. Another guest was being carried from the room, the dark cloth of his trousers darker around the crotch and the engorged tip of his tongue showing between the open oval of his mouth like the shoot of a plant rooted in the fertile density of his skull.

Sansiega sipped at her wine. Around the table she counted the faces unmarked by the eating of the third course. One ... two ... three... four ... five. In all the rest there were swellings, huge beneath the flushed, tightened skin, distorting to unrecognizability the faces with which she had grown acquainted in her quarter-hour at the table.

Only the eyes could have remained unchanged in the sting-swollen faces, but the eyes were slitted or closed against the pain. The glasses rose and fell, tinkling. Some could barely drink, even, the water sliding back along the throats of the glasses to bloated lips that opened narrowly, very narrowly for it.

Another guest tipped, slid beneath the edge of the table and the servants moved in on her; something began to jerk and jump in the chest of a man whose lips and left cheek were swollen hugely, and he bent back to vomit, one hand slipping below the table for his stomach. The pulses came, hammered up from his guts into his throat, but his mouth could not open wide enough. The right, unswollen cheek ballooned on the pressure of the vomit; between the thin slot in his lips it squirted vividly; Sansiega heard it spatter inside the vase, hollow-sounding; his hands rose, clawing at his face, at the swollen flesh of his mouth, and a further rhythm was written into the heaving of his body, written back against his guts from his throat; his body twisted for air and then, suddenly, as though it had been pulled away, his chair tipped up beneath him and he went over backwards.

Sansiega wondered at her calm, listening to the thrash of the man's struggles, hidden from her by the bulk of the table. He's choking, she said to herself, and yet you do nothing, wish to do nothing. She lifted her wine-glass and sipped. No-one did nothing. It did not seem as though they would serve the fourth course until the man was dead. He seemed a long time in dying. She listened, felt the tremors of his dying in the floor through her feet, and watched the faces around the table bloat with the stings. Such pain! She could not imagine it and yet it was so near to her. She thought, if it were Alanna that suffered thus, I could imagine it and I would feel it, perhaps. There would be a sympathy. That is what love would give to me: the power to suffer with her I loved. But these people, they are strangers. They are little to me, become nothing in their suffering. And surely they have chosen it, or else how could they endure it?

The floor beneath her feet became still. He was dead, the man. Servants stooped for his body, carried him from the room, one holding his head straight and forward by the nape of the neck, that the dribble of vomit between the lips from the charged, ballooned cheeks might not soil the floor. Vomit covered the black front of the man's dinner-jacket, glistening smears and strings of an autographic ideogram for death that could be given many sounds but only one sense.

Behind the servants carrying the dead man another servant walked with the vase into which the dead man had vomited. The vase was black and glittered with abstract patterns in gold and silver. She thought, it was his vase. He chose it, for this. For his death.

When the body had been carried out the trolleys of the fourth course were wheeled in. The covers this time were of arched glass, ribbed and veined in the shape of huge oak-leaves. Through the glass could be seen, on long oval dishes of white porcelain, patches, splashes of vivid colour, reds and oranges and yellows, like gouts of alien blood. A white-gloved hand was laid to the leaf-stem of each cover; on the speakers the bell slowly tolled four times; the voice said, "Fried poison-arrow frog;" the covers were lifted back: on the oval plates, patterned skins lifted glistening to the chandeliers, little frogs, fried, with fore-limbs stretched wide from their bodies and hind-limbs straight.

The sides of the trolleys were run back, plates lifted to receive, tipped from a narrow-bladed, long-necked spatula, the frogs, one to a plate, little crucifixions carried and laid to the table.

Sansiega was sickened, suddenly, at the gapped circle of frogs, splayed against the white porcelain of the plates, at the swollen heads bent over them, waiting.

The last plate was laid in place and the guests picked up knives and forks, sharp and small and ivory-handled. There was uncertainty: the frogs were so small on the plates, splayed before the waiting, silver-fanged hands! the pain in the guests' heads so great, so befuddling! The heads turned and swung, looking for her or him who could devise a means of eating. It was seen — the fork half-speared to frog-shoulder or thigh, holding the creature steady for the careful, slicing knife — copied, the three or four who knew foci of the concentration of those, second-slower, who knew not.

Now, scraps of frog were being raised to sting-deformed mouths that opened irregularly for them; the white meat, Sansiega saw, was ignored by some, who worked steadily at the flaying of the tiny cadavers before them, lifting triangles of the bright skin to their mouths and chewing slowly and carefully; others skeletonized, eating everything but the delicate bones, the tips of their knives surgically deft in the millimetre gaps of the radii and ulnae, fibulae and tibiae, on the miniature keep of the skull. The eyes, even, they ate, these ones, cutting at the outer muscles of the sockets and working the eyeballs free, to be speared like tiny berries on the sharp little forks and lifted, bleeding thin fluid, to the all-eating mouths.

Many mouths could neither open nor close properly, and trails of saliva, coloured variously with blood and batrachodermic pigments, crept on many chins, dripped, slowly, to the surface of the table. Save for the working of the jaws, the moist hiss and sough of difficult breath and the low, occasional, metallic stutter of fork and knife on porcelain, there was silence, broken once, twice, three times, when there came as before a revolt of guts against throat and mouth, and three bodies jerked and hammered, and three guests bent back for the vases set behind their chairs.

Of the three, one asphyxiated, an old man whose light body was easy in the hands of the servants: the other two, a woman and a man, sat exhausted in their places over their unfinished frogs, eyes closed against the pain of the meal. Theirs were the first plates taken away, carried individually by servants from the room; the other plates, later, were stacked into the interior of trolleys wheeled in for them (the skeletons, the flayed little cadavers tipped sideways from the plates with a minimal turn of the wrist into waste-dishes atop the trolleys). The trolley-sides were run closed, the waste-dishes capped, and the trolleys wheeled from the room as another guest, a man, began to vomit, leaning back in his chair for his vase, his thrown-back profile, beyond the stretched line of the throat, swollen huge with stings.

Sansiega counted around the table. Forty-three from fifty-five, and many of the forty-three sat shrunken, huddled in their chairs as though against great cold. Some shivered, eyes closed, hands lifted to their faces, their throats, fingers touching and stroking the surfaces of the great sting-swellings that rose like fruit embedded in their flesh. A woman's dark head rose and fell on a heart-beat-and-a-half rhythm, as though she mourned herself; a man, eyes closed and leaking bright tears, rocked side to side, side to side in his chair, hands collared loosely on his throat; spittle and vomit glittered or shone dully on many chins; many guests had bitten back the pain into lips or cheeks so deeply that blood had flowed; the teeth of one woman were embedded still in her lower lip, white in red, like a key twisted firmly into a door that held back pain, and blood flowed and dripped from the point of her chin to her pale dress, staining it wider, wider, second by second; the shirts and dresses of many others were similarly stained, and the sweet musks of perfume and aftershave were underlaid by the smell of blood or soured by the smell of vomit and sweat.

The trolleys of the fifth course were wheeled in.

Atop each rested two great crystal-capped bowls, but the course was not served at once. Instead each guest (save, of course, for Sansiega and Alanna) was attended by a servant, who bent whispering in her ear. Some heads were shaken, most were nodded; the bowls were uncapped; the sides of the trolleys were run open, dishes lifted up; on the speakers the bell tolled five times, slowly, and the epicene voice said (was there weariness in it, or an irony, this last time, a suggestion of mockery in a breathy-voiced vowel, the hint of a parodied, poetical rhythm in the syllabification?), "A trifle made of the berries of the several varieties of belladonna, of cuckoo-pint, and of the flowers of monkshood."

Wide silver spoons sank into the thick, sugary flesh of trifles topped with pale, swirled cream and delicate arabesques of powdered chocolate that wheeled and spiralled on a central, terraced peak, and gouged up (slow sucking sounds, a final, small *tchlop*) portions, which were turned and dropped into the dishes (again, smaller, *tchlop*), where the inner strata of the desert were revealed: layers, divided by thin, bright seams of custard, of tight-packed berries, red and yellow and black, in transparent jelly. The portions of trifle shook faintly, fat and heavy in the dishes like sugared organs, lungs or livers gouged from the blind, cream-skinned beasts crouched in the bowls. The dishes were carried and laid to the places of those who had nodded to the whispering. A man rose unsteadily in his chair, arms grasped at his belly, and turned slowly, blinking, stooped. A servant stepped to him and took his elbow, tugged, gently, and guided him towards a door, almost at which the single servant was joined by two more, who took the man by second elbow and waist, almost lifting him from his feet.

When the laying-out of plates was complete, spoons were taken up and the fifth course began, slowly, and for many with great difficulty. Those who had refused it sat, filled with pain like earth-hollows with dew, or flowers that cupped dulling blood on a field of slaughter, and bowed and grasped the reality of their pain to themselves.

Another man, and a woman (her spoon rattled on the lip of her dish), rose unsteadily from their places and servants stepped to them, smoothly, swiftly, and took their arms (at the first touch the swift, precise urgency of the servants' movements became slow, careful, as though pain filtered deadeningly through the cloth of the sufferer's clothing) and led them from the room; a man, face ripe and huge and shining with stings, began to vomit: a berry clung to the underside of his lip for a moment like a round little parasite, then dropped and bounced off the table as he swung on his chair for his vase; another woman had risen from her dessert, arms clasped on her belly, mouth shaped on silent agony; she was led from the room.

Few finished the final course: spoon half-raised or half-dropped from or to the trifle, the guests paused, as though reminded of or remembering something very important; then the spoons were laid down carefully in the dishes and they shrank on their seats into the waiting. The servants began to take the dishes away. Another man rose and was led away. Sansiega looked to Alanna and found that her eyes were already turned to her. Now, as their eyes met, Alanna bent towards her. Her hair smelt faintly of oil and flowers. She said, "Tell me, have you ever seen a dinner party like this?"

Sansiega shook her head. Alanna smiled strangely, then her eyes focussed up and away from Sansiega's face. She said, "Look, can you see that moth? There must be a window open somewhere and it's got in. How it loves the light!"

Sansiega looked up and saw a scrap of white spiralling beneath a chandelier.

"A muth?"

"No, a moth. Moth."

"OK. A moth. Moth. O!"

"It'll get tired soon. Fall. Watch it."

They watched the moth twist and spiral in the light. Twice it seemed exhausted, and fell away, but it had a long way to fall and each time it recovered before it came to the level of the floor or table, and lifted again on the urgency of its desire. As it fell for a third time, spinning, a party of women, some of them carrying instrument cases (a cello, three violins), came into the room; when Sansiega looked for the moth again she could not see it on the air; it must have fallen and be lying unknown somewhere, on the table, on the floor, crushed, perhaps, under the women's neat, shining shoes as the women walked to the raised stand at one end of the room, the oval platform she had seen when she first came into the room.

Servants stepped ahead of the women, drew the covers from high-. backed, velvet-cushioned chairs, from a discrete nest of drums and a microphone stand, the draped shapes she had wondered at, a little, long before. Drums and microphone were old-looking, she thought; the women's dresses were in the style of the thirties, and their hair, too, and even their make-up. None wore jewellery, except the singer (she was adjusting the height of the microphone, bending her head to it and breathing "huh, huh" as though it were the neck of a pet swan, say, lifted erect to her in greeting) whose wrist was circled with a thin bracelet of pearls.

The others, unadorned, were opening their instrument cases. The locks clicked sharply, like bones, and the instruments, taken out carefully, seemed like little shining corpses, mummified, and varnished against decay. The drummer sat down behind her drums and took up her sticks. The violinists, the cellist, clipped little wire-trailing discs to the bodies of their instruments, Frankensteins, she thought, attaching life-electrodes to their soon-to-live monsters. From the instruments the wires disappeared through little holes in the surface of the platform.

The singer went "huh, huh" again into her microphone and signalled (fingers pinched, twisting clockwise) to a servant standing by a wall, who swung open a section of the wall and made adjustments to the dials of a control panel.

Far louder, "huh, huh", and there was a crash of sound, a rolling series of detonations, from the drummer, her hands dancing up-down-up-down, curved through the drum nest. The violins squawked, sharply, almost hurting her ears, and the cellist sawed at her instrument, a long stroke over strangely adjusted strings that produced a deep, throbbing sound, half-groan, half-snore. The cellist's left hand glided up and down on the neck of the cello and the sound swooped and fell weirdly. Sansiega felt it through the soles of her feet, shivering in the floor. Hands ran up and down on the necks of the violins, the cello, turning the keys, tightening, loosening strings, and the drums exploded again, the dancing hands curving back and forth across the taut, resounding circle-faces.

The dishes of the final course had been cleared away completely now and servants were busy around the table, busy with decanters of fatly lustrous spirits that flooded briefly into balloon-like glasses where nods were made to whispering, busy with thick silver cigar-cases that flashed dully as they were opened to reveal tight double rows of cigars. Lighters sprang and flared (faces leapt bigger, taking deeper colour from the light of the flame, then died back into the half-shadow) and after a few moments slow white smoke dribbled from the grotesque, sting-ripe lips and began to float and thin across the table.

The smoke smelt rich and strange and strong, like incense in a darkened temple or the blood-quenched ashes of witch-herbs. When the glasses had been filled and the cigars lit, each servant, save him who stood beside the control panel, watchful for the signals of the singer, left the room.

And now the singer glanced around the members of her group and nodded to the servant standing by the control panel. The servant made a final adjustment to a dial, closed the door of the control panel and left the room. It was going to be very loud, Sansiega could tell. The slightest touch, movement of the instruments, even the singer's breathing, sounded on the speakers, hung and was overlaid and overlaid, like thin, faded, patterned cloths being tugged flat and laid to the surface of a table, layer on layer.

The playing began.

First, the drummer, laying down a slow one-one beat, a huge invisible heart thumping on the air, subverting the rhythms of Sansiega's own body; then the cellist shifted on her chair, her left hand curling on the neck of the cello; the bow swung to the strings (its faint bounce and settle boomed on the speakers over the thump of the drums), and she

61

began to play, short, vibrato'd notes, sawn strongly into the instrument, and huge on the speakers as the fall of sky-high iron towers in a dead wilderness of ice.

The smell of the cigar smoke sharpened and swelled in Sansiega's nostrils and she felt her lungs swell and draw it deep, once, twice. The table beneath the fingers of one resting hand, the chair beneath her buttocks and thighs, the floor beneath the soles of her feet, all three shook, broke almost to the notes of the cello and beat of the drums; the bare skin of her face and neck and hands flinched and tightened to the sound; her ears filled and burst with it, over and over; she wondered, almost, why she could not see the music around her, and gradually she did, a thickening purple mist rising from tumbled blocks of sea-smoothed black stone, the mist touched (the violins, dabbed, dabbed, dabbed, began to underline the cello's notes with sharp, squawked chords) with bright, vertical tendrils of yellow and white, the whole shot suddenly (the singer growled into the microphone) through with rays of sick, turning violet, axis'd on the room's eight corners, as though the room were a submarine cavern sifted by the tentacles of kraken.

The smoke of the cigars hung on the air, thin and shifting, thickening; on the other side of the table the faces of the guests were softened by it; the brandy glasses rose and fell through it like crystal moons, oceaned internally with the rich, cold ichor of dead gods or demons: imposed on this scene, seen through it and beneath it, the visioned notes of the music, the weaving purple/white/yellow/violet/black of the voice and violins and cello and drums.

The singer growled again, a thick, roughened sound that simultaneously swamped and lifted the sawing notes of the cello and the light, sharp strokes of the violins: on the neck of the microphone her right hand tightened and she tilted it back a little, presenting the round, false-halo'd ear closer to her mouth, which yawned on it, wide and round: Sansiega could see the glint of the teeth, the moist, darkened red of buccal tissues, the movement of the fat tongue, lifting towards the alveolus; and the singer began to chant, thickly and incomprehensibly, shifting her delivery between the creaky notes of a groan and the smooth whisper of a sigh, and the notes of the violins and cello tightened and accelerated beneath her voice; beneath them, the giant heart-beat of the drums stuttered and began to race, a headlong beat sewn with little arrhythmic clusters like debris spinning on a flood-accelerated river.

It was cruel, ugly, a music of pain, a calculated aural *Grand Guignol*; through the purple, white/yellow lanced mist, the turning violet rays darkened towards blue; the violins, one by one, loosened from the notes of the cello, remoras from the rough belly of a shark, and now laid down a continual strident chord, sawn again and again from the violins' rigid shining bodies, a shrill ocean through which the chanting and cello swooped and hunted above the shifting, tumbled black blocks of the drums like giant carnivorous fish.

Above, the chandeliers dimmed a little more and servants came back into the room. In the gloom it took Sansiega a moment to see that their clothes and hands and heads glistened, and a moment longer to see why. The servants wore long aprons and gloves, extending almost to the shoulder, of transparent plastic, and thigh boots of the same stuff, and shower-caps of it, pulled tight and low to the scalp. Their eyes swung moistly above surgical masks.

They began to file around the table and she saw that the toes of their boots were grey and bluntly faceted. Beside her, Alanna shifted in her seat, and she was about to look towards her when four of the servants moved, very quickly, seizing a man who sat six, seven places away from them by his shoulders and arms and wrenching him backwards, off his chair, and standing him on the floor, where they began to beat him, furiously and scientifically, short, chopped punches into the face and neck and ears and kidneys and belly; almost at once, from the swollen tissues of the face and mouth, blood began to flow.

It splattered to the rhythm of the punches, patterning the transparent plastic of the aprons and gloves and boots and shower-caps, lightly at first, then thicker and thicker. The man began to fold under the blows, falling to the floor, though slowly, for the punches came at him so quickly that he was almost supported by them.

When he was fully down the boots began to thud silently home into his body in the rush of the music, the toe-caps sinking deep into his back and kidneys and stomach and genitals. The other servants stood in a loose circle around the table, eyes flickering between the beating and the other guests. The beaten man was foetus'd now under the kicks, head and knees brought together, arms bound over the skull. Shortly, or already, he would be unconscious. Shortly, he would be dead.

On the platform, as the beating began, the singer had jerked the microphone stand hard against her body and begun to shriek, half in triumph, half in empathetic agony, and around her voice the cello and violins and drums were half-infected with the rhythms of the blows, half, it seemed, providing a rhythm for those performing the beating.

Sansiega, open-mouthed and staring, barely felt Alanna's first tug at her elbow. A second came, and a third, and she turned to Alanna, who jerked her head up and sideways, as though to say, "Let's go", and rose from her chair.

Sansiega stood up too. Alanna leaned to her and shouted in her ear.

On the fourth repetition, Sansiega understood.

*Don't touch any blood or body fluids.*

Alanna started to walk away around the table. As Sansiega started to follow her, the singer fell silent, bowing her head beside the microphone stand (the darkened violet rays withdrew like tentacles; only a faint glow remained in each corner), and one of the violinists stood up and began to solo over and around the notes of the cello (in the purple mist, the tendrils of yellow and white sharpened and scrawled, multiplied and ran like webs). She thought, I will be caught up in them, and stopped, looking up and around her at the vision, but Alanna was looking back over her shoulder for her and stepped back and caught at her hand and pulled her on.

As they moved around the table other guests were beginning to stand, though they didn't move away from the table, only turned and watched the servants, some of whom began to feed weight from foot to foot, waiting. Half the guests at the table, more than half, were standing now, and one, a man, moved, stepping away from it, looking left and right at the other guests, jerking his hands to them, as though to say, come on, come on.

Servants jumped at him at once; boots, fists, to groin, belly, face; and he was down and being kicked to death. Now other guests moved, those nearest to him at first, running for the gaps in the circle, then all of those standing were running at the circle of plastic-wet servants, and the circle was broken in half-a-dozen places, the servants ganging three, four, five to a victim and the rest of the guests running, staggering, for the room's three exits. Alanna's hand tightened on Sansiega's and Alanna stopped, waiting for the guests to leave the room, which was now violent, there and there and there and there and there, with the beatings. Some of the guests fell as they tried to run: most found their feet again quickly, fear-driven; two or three lay where they had fallen; a few more began to crawl as quickly as they were able for the exits.

Alanna's hand tightened again and Sansiega was tugged forward for the nearest, past a crawling man. The seat of his trousers was darkly stained and Sansiega plugged her breath to the fresh stink of diarrhoea. Behind them, the music had accelerated with vile glee. The singer howled and she looked back. The cigar smoke had curtained on the rush of escape and evasion; here and there, from dropped cigars, threads of it rose, straightening; a few seats were still occupied, those who sat in them slumped forward on the table; on the far side of the table the four servants of the first beating were straightening themselves, standing away from death, the slick, flexing surfaces of their aprons and gloves running and shining with blood; the other servants were bent still to their labour, beating bodies like blacksmiths at anvils, hammering life-metal to death-metal; the singer howled again, but even as she did the image woken in Sansiega's head by the smoke of the cigars (tentacles lashing forth from the eight corners of the room) was fading; she was tugged through the door.

Outside the room, they found themselves in a wide, marble-floored corridor. Right, and Sansiega thought they would come to the gardens she had seen at the front; left, and there were the first steps of what seemed to be a long flight of stairs.

Across from them, at waist-height on the white-plastered wall, there were rayed splashes of blood, five wide, wet flowers, glistening, from which red drops had collected themselves and run down the wall like the strokes of bloody-fingered hands, three- or four- or five- or witch-fingered. The guests helped out earlier by the servants lay beneath the flowers, heads pointed to the wall, limbs loose and turned or twisted at strange angles: man, woman, man, man, woman.

Alanna released Sansiega's hand as they looked, then turned and began to walk to the right. As Sansiega followed her she saw that the faces and foreheads of the dead were crushed and oozed slow, cold blood. She looked away, but the murders were picturing themselves against her will in her head.

She walked to the right, stepping carefully between splatters of blood lying on the floor. Alanna was standing with her back to her at the top of a flight of stairs. There was a wind blowing down the corridor. The green hem of Alanna's dress jerked and flapped faintly around her legs and the black silk trimming seemed almost alive, stirring against her body like tiny snakes or the prophetic, living letters of a qabbalistic alphabet.

Alanna half-turned, looking back. Her hair fluttered around her face. One thick strand danced and trembled around an eye and she lifted a hand and pulled it back.

Sansiega ran to her. Close to her, she felt the wind blowing harder. Alanna shouted (but Sansiega understood only the movements of her lips in the huge pollution of the music), "Come on," and turned back and started down the stairs again. Sansiega followed her, having to run a little to keep pace.

Half way down the stairs they passed a woman working her way down backwards on hands and knees. Sansiega thought her face must have been beautiful, before. But now one cheek was swollen tumorously red, the skin smooth and shiny, and the other cheek glistened saltily with tears.

Blood and vomit had dried in flat, flaking lines on her chin and she stank of vomit and sweat.

They reached the bottom of the stairs, and turned left. Sansiega recognized the paintings on the wall. It was the corridor leading from the entrance.

The two men were gone and there was a cold wind blowing through the open door.

Sansiega said, only having to half-shout now over the music, "Wait!"

She went through the door through which she had seen the man take her leather jacket. Beyond the door was a small room. Coats were heaped on the floor everywhere. Her foot crunched on a glasses case and a key-ring sat fatly on the sleeve of a leather jacket, not hers. Someone seemed to have been going through the pockets.

She started to turn the coats over, looking for her jacket.

Some of the coats were wet.

She sniffed her hands and wrinkled her nose.

She saw her jacket. It was in a corner, crumpled as though thrown there. She kicked a space clear on the floor and wiped her hands dry against the carpet.

Her jacket hadn't been pissed on.

She felt in the pockets. Some money was missing.

Otherwise, all her stuff was there.

She left the room.

They left the house.

# *Twelve*

She had said, when they said goodbye at the consulate, "I have to see you again." Six simple words, but Sansiega thought they were the most powerful she had ever heard. They seemed to buzz inside her head like insects, like huge tawny bees.

And she had replied, "Me too," and now she had a day, an hour, a place, when she and she would meet again. She thought of it as an island, a black-cliffed enchantress's island, green-groved and towering, towards which she rode the warring waves of an oceanic river, the river of time, broad and blue and sun-blessed, but the thin spray of the waves was cold on her face and she knew that below her the depths of the river were dark and freezing and infinite.

After they left the consulate, they walked a little in the garden, and then sat on the rim of the fountain. Alanna began to pluck leaves from a small tree growing near the fountain and floated them in the current-busy basin, watching them turn and vanish into the darkness further out.

Light glittered on the water.

The air was cold.

They began to talk, shivering, in low, half-whispering voices, fitting the words around the irregular notes of the fountain's silver glossolalia. From the consulate, as they talked, every so often they could hear screaming, and several times there were loud crashes, as though of heavy objects falling through glass, and always, the faint growling of the music.

"Why did you want to kill me?"

"Because I hated you."

"You had never met me."

"I hated you."

"I don't understand. You're crazy."

"No, not crazy."

"Why did you want to do it?"

"I hated you."

Sansiega said nothing for a time.

She said, "I think that I know why you hated me. It's crazy. I have loved you for a long time."

"You have loved me?"

"Yes. I have loved you for a long time. Since 1989. You don't know anything about me, and you tried to kill me. I was a student of criminology at Deusto University, in Bilbao. I wrote my ... I don't know what it is in English. In Spanish, *mi tesis*. I wrote it about women in the European police forces. I wrote in it a lot about you. I wrote to you several times."

"I don't remember."

"It doesn't matter. You replied to me. A few questions. It is easy to forget. I was in love with you."

"Not with me. With my picture. My image."

"OK, with your picture. With your image. I often wondered if I would love you if I met you in reality. Now I have."

A brief silence.

"And do you? Love me?"

*"Mas que la hostia."*

"What does that mean?"

"It's Spanish. It's very rude. It means, yes, I love you a fucking lot. Why are you laughing?"

"It sounded funny when you swore."

"Don't you like it?"

"Yes, I liked it. It's very sexy. Swear to me some more."

"No. I want to tell you about *el Rey*. About the King."

"Tell me about the King then."

"I will. It sounds a bit funny. Bloody funny."

"Fucking funny."

"Fucking funny. I think what he does, he uses a book in it."

"What do you mean?"

"He uses a book. There is a book that I know. I think he has read it too, and he uses it for ideas. How do you say it? He is *based* in the book."

"I understand. What book is it?"

"It is a book that is only available in Basque. It is quite old now. I suppose it is a crime book, but it is strange too. It is a feminist book. A religious book. But not a Christian book. *Es un libro de la Diosa.* You know, *de la Diosa?*"

"Yes. In English, it means, of the Goddess."

"OK, of the Goddess. A book of the Goddess."

"What is it called?"

"In Basque, *Berria Atalantea*. In Spanish, that is *La Atalanta Nueva*. In English, I suppose, 'The New Atalanta'."

"And what is it about?"

"It's about ... *un jabilí. Una cacería de un jabilí.* The hunting of a pig."

"I think you probably mean the hunting of a boar."

"No, of a pig. Not of a bore. It is an interesting book."

"No, not of a bore as in 'uninteresting', of a boar as in 'pig'. They're spelt differently. But don't worry, 'pig' is OK."

"OK."

"Do you have this book?"

"Yes. I have it with me in England."

"And are you certain about what you're saying?"

"Yes. He isn't always based in the book, but usually, when he kills, it is like a killing in the book."

"Doesn't he ever run out?"

"I'm sorry?"

"How many killings are there in the book? How many murders?"

"Oh, lots. Fucking lots. You're laughing at me again!"

# *Thirteen*

"Would you like some more tea?"

"Yes, please."

It was very quiet. Sansiega could hear the tea glugging loudly into the cup, and the ring of the spoon sounded very sharp as Alanna stirred in the sugar and handed the cup to her.

"Thank you."

"And have as many biscuits as you want. You like sweet things, don't you?"

"Yes. Too much."

"Don't say that. You are my guest. It would offend me."

"Really?"

"No, I'm joking. Here."

"Thank you."

On the clear yellow carpet of the floor, the shadows of leaves danced and shook.

Hundreds of them.

There was an oak tree outside the window. A quite young one, but already very tall. A minute before, she had seen a bird hopping amongst the leaves, a bird-shadow, but it had seemed alive, a living shadow hopping amongst the dancing leaf-shadows on the floor. And when the bird had flown away, her eyes had risen involuntarily to the window, and she had seen it fly past, travelling too fast to identify.

She picked up a biscuit and said, "This is very English, isn't it?"

"This?"

"Drinking tea and eating biscuits."

"I don't know. I think it was, but not nowadays. All that is disappearing, I think. But I'm not sure if it was ever very English. What is English?"

"If you don't know, then I do not."

"So, what is Spanish?"

"I don't know. I never want to be Spanish, when I live in Spain."

"What do you want to be?"

"Nothing. Oh, yes, I would like to be Basque, but that is impossible."

"But you were born in Bilbao."

"But that didn't mean I was Basque, just that I was Bilbaina. My family was not Basque."

"What does that mean?"

"Bilbaina? It means someone, something from Bilbao."

"And that is what you are?"

"Yes. Or what I was."

"Now ... it doesn't matter. When you've finished your tea, let's go and see something."

"What?"

"When you've finished."

"Look. I have."

"OK."

Alanna stood up. How tall she was! As she walked towards the door the cool cloth of her legs from the knees down was patterned with the shadows of the leaves. Sansiega set her cup and saucer down on the low tea-table and stood up herself. As she followed Alanna from the room she glanced out of the window at the tree whose leaves she had watched dance on the floor.

She stopped and stood looking at the tree.

From some of the lower branches little shapes seemed to be hanging. They looked like people, but they were too small.

Like dolls.

She would ask about it later.She walked out of the room.

Alanna said, "Upstairs. Race?"

"But —"

"Yes or no?"

"Yes."

She tried to cheat, throwing herself, her arms around the slim waist, trying to hold Alanna back. Her victim rocked, side to side, and kicked backwards with calculated chops of her heels. She danced her shins safe; Alanna jerked forward, climbed one, two, three steps, then they fell forward, together, Sansiega still clasped on the slim, strong waist.

"Ow!"

Then they were both giggling, and fighting each other up on hands and knees, Sansiega hauling herself higher on Alanna's body (hand on a cool *nucha*, the work and relaxation of muscles and sinews in a hard-held forearm).

Alanna said, "If I stop, will you?"

"No."

"You started it. Ouch!"

"I'll — *¡jo!* — finish it. When..."

When they reached the top of the stairs, both were hot, flushed, laughing.

"I can't stand," said Alanna. "Your knee."

"My knee? *¡Tu codo! ¡Los dos!*"

"I'm bruised all over."

"Me, a broken rib, at the least."

"You started it."

"I had to."

"Owww! See?"

She stood up, groaning.

"And what about me? But I don't complain. *Soy dura.*"

"*¿Tu?*"

"Yooooo. Ooooo. Nooo. Ooooo."

"Stop complaining and open the door."

"When you let go of my arm."

"Well, I don't want to. Tell me why I should?"

"Because it's hurting me. You're hurting me."

"And you don't like it?"

"Of course — no!"

"No?"

"Yes."

"Yes to 'no'?"

"Yes."

"OK."

And the door was opened.

Beyond it, the room was very long and tall, dimly lit through the half-drawn curtains of three, four, five, windows. Sansiega looked around her, feeling the hard wood of the floor through the soles of her shoes. For a moment she thought the hunched, brooding shapes were alive, but then she saw that they were video game consoles, black and massive and silent. By the doorway Alanna's arm moved and there was a click. Eerily, the screens, the faces of the consoles came alive and began to crawl with vivid little chips of light, green and red and purple and yellow and white.

Another click and the ceiling fluoros glowed and hidden speakers began to growl softly.

"Well?" said Alanna.

"*Juegos de video.* Video games."

"*Muy bien.* Have you played them before?"

"One time, maybe. Maybe more. I don't remember."

"Have a look."

"Show me a game."

"OK. How about this one? They had one of these on the Ark. It's ancient. But it's one of my favourites. Look."

She took hold of the console's joystick and the screen began to flower with colour as she guided a triangular spaceship through a subterranean alien city. The spaceship rose and danced through flowering explosions, spitting back white and red missiles at the ray-gun emplacements and alien fighters that menaced it.

She said, "D'you see how you do it? See, this for the force-field, yeah, and there are these missiles, like this, see? Two types, one's semi-intelligent, but you have to be careful with them, and this is the laser. *Tshu-tshu! Tshu-tshu!* It's great, yeah? D'you wanna go?"

"Yeah, OK."

"I'll just get this defender cluster out of the way, yeah ... OK, all yours ... good, yeah ... good ... brilliant ... look out ... uh-oh!"

And despite herself, somehow, Sansiega found the game begin to grip her attention. The colours, somehow, the bright, moving shapes, even the wilfully ugly music, all these were part of it. And Alanna, leaning on the console at her side, restless, bouncing on the balls of her feet, encouraging her, groaning as she almost spun the ship into a blind tunnel, yeah, good .. yeah, yeah ... and, "Shit!"

Alanna laughed and said, "You should say, 'Pardon my French'."

"Why?"

"It's what you say. It's a sort of joke. No, don't bother with this one again. There are lots more. Look, what about this one?"

There was something strange in her voice as she said this. Sansiegea glanced at her, then at the black screen of the video game. Alanna punched one of the buttons set beneath the screen. Something screamed gratingly inside the console, as though an iron nerve had been twisted. A vague golden outline appeared on the screen, glittering. It hardened, sharpened, becoming the head and chest of a lion.

After a moment, as Sansiega had guessed it would, it roared — *la MGM*; a thick string twanged fruitily and a burning arrow had sprouted between its eyes. It melted like golden wax into a pool of blood, over which a second outline shimmered, a swaying human figure, solidifying, sharpening into a pelvising young Elvis Presley with microphone stand and quiff. Blood splashed around the figure's blue suede shoes, but the musical accompaniment to its gyrations was a distorted version of "King Creole". After a couple of seconds, something white flashed in an upper corner of the screen and a white lavatory pan on a golden chain had arced left-right and taken quiff and head from the Elvis's shoulders.

Blood fountained from the neck-stump and the figure, gyrating as wildly as ever, sank into the deepening pool. "King Creole" bubbled into silence; a second passed; the console screamed again and something began to rise from the pool of blood: the shell of a black scallop, opening with a teeth-setting screech of rusting metal to reveal within, draping its nakedness with the steaming entrails of the men and women sprawled slaughtered at its feet, the crowned, knife-wielding figure of a grotesquely-muscled man. Eyes flashed behind the pentagrammic peep-holes of a domino and the knife lifted and slashed once, twice, three times. The image fell away into sections like slashed flesh from the darkness behind.

Another electronic scream and words were burning against the blackness:

## THE SLAUGHTER KING™

The words faded and the rusting walkways and stairs of a disused inner city warehouse or factory appeared on the screen. More screams, and the naked figures of men and women were running to and fro on the walkways. The crowned figure of the scallop shell, dressed now in flamboyant leather, leapt into view with simian agility. The knife flashed and the limbs and head of a naked woman flew in all directions with *tlunks* and gratings of parting muscle and bone; the crowned figure leapt for its next victim.

Sansiega wrinkled her nose.

"How do you play it?" she asked.

Almost reluctantly, Alanna took her eyes from the screen (another naked figure flew apart, its limbs and head showering to the filthy concrete floor of the warehouse).

"What?"

"How do you play it?"

"Oh. Like this."

She took hold of one of the console's joysticks.

A tiny figure, almost completely hidden under a Clouseau raincoat, puffing on an enormous meerschaum and peering into an enormous magnifying glass, bumbled onto the screen.

"This is the policeman."

More limbs showered to the warehouse floor; the head bounced after them like rubber down the stairs, level to level.

"You have to chase him. Like this."

The raincoated figure hopped onto a stair and began to run up it.

"Watching out, of course" — the figure hopped again as the head bounced toward it — "for the bits and pieces."

Another naked figure came apart in flurry of knife-strokes. The tiny policeman skipped and hopped narrowly clear of the falling fragments. Above, the crowned figure waved its knife in defiance and leapt for another victim.

"It's horrible."

"Yes. Shall I switch if off?"

"Yes. Switch if off."

Alanna pushed a button and the screen iris'd-out to black.

"And *now*," she said — and paused.

"What?"

"Fancy dipping your wick?"

# *Fourteen*

"Is it done?"

"No. Not as yet. Technical hitch."

"Meaning?"

"Meaning our mutual friend — if you'll pardon the solecism — is having second thoughts."

"Twist his balls, then."

"If we were able to, we would. But he's had his eye on that commissionaireship since well before the last election and J's worried that if we push him too hard that he may decide that snout in trough for him tomorrow wins out over jam for H.M.G. today."

"Go to J and tell him to do whatever it takes. We've got enough on him to keep his nose to the grindstone."

"We have?"

"We have. Or will have. Just go to J and tell him. I'll see to the rest."

"OK, fine. I'll ring him and arrange something for after lunch."

# *Fifteen*

The pool was on the ground floor, in a huge white room at the rear of the house. It was round and very big and blue and seemed very deep. There was a big stereo in one corner, and racks of necro-industrial CDs. Alanna said, "We'll play something later, if you like."

She led Sansiega to the changing room. Inside it, there was a long wardrobe of scented wood, filled with swimming costumes of every size and shape and colour.

Sansiega chose a single-piece in low, smouldering gold; Alanna one similar in dark, dark blue.

As they had chosen they had joked and stood close, nudging and pinching and slapping at each other; when the choices were made they fell silent and found separate corners in which, backs turned, to undress and dress.

Outside the dressing room, by the pool, they walked in opposite directions and stopped and turned to face each other with the pool's full width between them. The costume Sansiega wore had over each flank three long slots, horizontal on the left, vertical on the right, through which the white of her skin shone like milk against the golden cloth; in the dark, dark blue of the costume of Alanna, here and there, there were embroidered salamanders, sewn of deep red silk, with little crystal eyes that flashed double over and over as Alanna moved.

They stood with cold expressionless faces and looked towards each other for what seemed like a very long time and then suddenly Alanna winked and Sansiega smiled and thought she was about to start laughing when Alanna, in a single flowing movement, arms following hands, and head and shoulders arms, and torso and hips head and shoulders, and legs torso and hips, and feet (the left a second after the right) legs, dove forward into the pool, and Sansiega, as though the grace of Alanna's dive whirled and sucked irresistibly on the air, dove forward herself into the clear deep water.

And screamed silently and hugely beneath it, for it was cold, very cold, icy, and seemed almost at once to suck sensation out of her, so that she felt as though she had become simplified, a creature merely of arms and legs and head and torso, without hands or feet or lips or nose or ears or toes or fingers. As she rose to the surface from the dive and sucked and gasped agonized on the air, her breath steamed and swirled on the surface of the water.

She trod water, feeling her strength drawn from her into the water, and looked for Alanna. To be in the water was already painful. Her ears were beginning to ache. She thrust and bounced on the hurting water, lifting her head to look around her into the water for Alanna.

And there, deep in the water, a distorted darker blue ripple against the blue of the pool bottom, swimming towards her, deep.

She gasped air greedily and thrust herself downwards into the dead, deadening cold.

Deep beneath the surface of the pool they met, urgently, swimming strongly towards each other, and each seized and held the other roughly. But there was no warmth in the embrace, and each felt the body of the other to be cold, very cold, like something dead, or something that had never known life.

Kicking, they rose towards the surface. As they broke it, they whistled in air, holding each other tightly and gazing into the other's face, very close, seeing the translucency of the wet, white, cold skin, where the blood had been sucked away, deeper, from the kisses of the water's myriad icy mouths.

Treading water, they turned slowly.

Sansiega released the straps of Alanna's swimming costume, Alanna those of Sansiega's: both did so slowly, with difficulty, almost unable to control numbed, unwilling fingers. Then they tugged, relaxing their embrace to allow the costumes to travel free of their bodies, slide down their legs and tangle momentarily in the kicking cycles of their feet.

Their embrace tightened again; below them, in the water, like the discarded pupal shells of huge aquatic insects, the swimming costumes hung on the water, slowly falling, and were low, smouldering gold and dark, dark blue; above, nipples were like eyes of metal or stone, hard in the flesh of the other; and neither smiled and each was frozen, turning in the pure, freezing water.

Alanna smiled, strangely, for her lips were numbed, and said something that Sansiega did not understand. And she repeated it and again Sansiega did not understand, and was surprised to find herself unsurprised as Alanna thrust down at her shoulders, sliding her smoothly into the freezing water, down the white cold body until the long thighs locked around her face.

The heat of Alanna's vulva, of her clitoris, was a shock. Almost, it seared her, burnt her, and she sealed her lips on it and fed forward her

78

tongue and Alanna's wet wide second mouth and hard clitoral teat were hot, too hot, and the cunnilingus was a delight that was an agony, but she could not break it, for her whole body demanded heat.

Drowning, she sucked, and in the universe there was nothing but the freezing water of the pool on her body and the heat of Alanna's sex melted to her mouth.

Consciousness returned not as sensation but as realization. The world was black, and she felt nothing, but her mind moved inside her head again.

She opened her eyes.

She was lying on the marble pool surround, sprawled breast-and-belly down with legs and arms turned wide from her body. There was no feeling in her skin, and she felt unable to move.

"You are still alive," said Alanna's voice from behind her, and she felt suddenly, between her scapulae, at or around the fourth dorsal vertebra, the exquisite sting of something very sharp and very hot. After a moment's pause, the something moved, travelling in a line down her spinal column, burning her and slicing her as it went. It lifted from her skin at the lip of the gluteal cleft, and after a moment touched her again between the scapulae, paused again, and re-traced its line down her spinal column, adding fire to the fire that burned there already, very sharply and thinly and precisely.

She tried to move, and could not.

The sharpness lifted again at the lip of her gluteal cleft, and touched her again after a moment between the scapulae. This third time, so intense was the pain that she felt sure a blade, having opened her skin, was splitting her spine in two.

She said, "No!", and tried to move, and could not.

"You are still alive," said Alanna's voice.

The sharpness lifted for the third time.

She waited for it to touch her between the scapulae again, and it did not. She smelt, suddenly, the tang of hot metal and the fumes of heated wine, and then her back was touched again, this time by many of the sharpnesses, symmetrically on the axis of her spine, half of them above her left scapula, half above her right.

They moved, tracing lines of pain down her back, as though the skin had been stripped away and white-hot blades cut against the moist red fabric of her dorsal muscles, from the midway of the trapezius, taking in the inner corner of the deltoid, half of the infra-spinatus, the exposed triangle of the rhomboideus major, and slowing, agonizingly, exquisitely, down the latissimus dorsi, until, almost, the first fringe of the gluteus medius. She screamed. The lines of agony were re-traced.

She screamed.

The lines of agony were re-traced.

A pause.

"Why do you hurt me like this?"

"Because I love you. Now, quiet; there is something else I have to do." The first drops of liquid on the lines of pain on her back felt like molten metal. She tried to scream but the muscles in her throat were twisted with the pain of it and would not obey her.

Alanna grunted delicately and released her bladder fully.

This time Sansiega was able to scream, thinly, like a kettle just coming to the boil. But the liquid pouring onto her back had been boiling for minutes, she was sure of it; and she could feel the white frozen skin between the sliced lines of the blades Alanna had used on her blistering up vividly into scalded flowers of vesication.

Urine splattered on the marble around her body. She could smell it, and a few drops of it were caught in her open mouth.

"Time," said Alanna, and the boiling flood dribbled into nothing.

There was a pause of some seconds while Alanna unclipped and threw clatteringly aside the heated bronze nails with which she had scratched Sansiega's back, pointed a remote control at the stereo and laid it aside, and strapped herself into a complicated harness of plastic and steel; and then Sansiega, whimpering, felt her thighs taken gently and lifted up and apart, and her cold vagina was filled smoothly and relentlessly with the warm, lubricated length of an enormous dildo.

"¡O! ¡Madre!" she said, and began, as the pleasure mounted inside her and climbed like soothing ice amongst the scalded patterns of her back, to weep.

# Sixteen

"Bless you," said Saphique as she lowered the silver tea-pot.

Then Sansiega, watching her lover as she added milk and sugar, saw what had happened, and when Saphique asked, "Lemon?" she could only nod with her gaze fixed on a patch of sunlight lying on the floor like thin multicoloured skin, for fear that if she spoke or met Saphique's eyes she would begin to giggle.

Saphique added a slice of lemon to the tea and handed the cup to her.

They had come to the house the previous night. It belonged to a friend of Saphique's, a producer who was working on a film in Morocco. They would be able to stay in it for nearly a fortnight. It was beautiful, very big, Georgian, and set in a wide garden with ponds and hedges and even a small maze. It was ringed by a brick wall and there was a long flight of stone steps leading up to the front door.

Sansiega had never met the producer.

Saphique wouldn't talk about her very much.

They were sitting in the solarium: floor of white marble and roof and walls of clear glass into which were set, like autumn leaves trapped in ice, patches of stained glass representing scenes from Greek mythology: anvil-weighted Hera hanging against infinity in bracelets of glittering gold; sea-robed Thetis sowing foam with an easy cast of a heavy arm; a sun-fired thread of metallic inlay passing from the spindle of long-fingered Clotho through the hands of rhabdometric Lachesis to the shears of monkshood-eyed Atropos; a mirror in a masculine hand in which a beautiful face is seen, ophiotrichated; bare-footed Artemis bending a silver bow.

Saphique said, "It's probably hay fever, from spending too much time in the garden."

"Hay fever?"

"Yes, from all the pollen."

"Ah, the pollen. No, it's not that."

"What is it then?"

"Oh, I think I have a cold coming on."

On the marble floor the patches of stained glass cast coloured shadows, distorted variously to the position of the sun. One lay almost at Sansiega's feet: stretching out her left foot she caught on the upper of her bare left foot, turning the foot right-left-right, Clotho-Lachesis-Atropos-Lachesis-Clotho-Lachesis-Atropos.

She said, "It is very beautiful here when the sun shines."

"Yes, very beautiful. But I am a little bored with the stained glass pictures. I have seen them too often."

Sansiega said, "No, they are very beautiful too."

Between her and Saphique there was a small table of dark wood, on which rested an oval silver tray, a silver sugar bowl, a silver milk-jug and a silver tea-pot.

They were a present to Saphique from the producer.

Each was decorated with an image of Saphique in one of her video rôles: on the silver tray she was Boudicca, bare breasts veined thinly with sweat, wrenching one-handed on the reins of a blade-axled chariot as her right hand, flung skywards, urged on a sky-line of tattooed warriors; on the sugar bowl she was the eponym of "The Lamia", stretched languorously against the curve of the bowl, yawning thirstily and beckoning to the viewer with a slim, sharp-nailed hand; on the milk-jug she was Medea, leaning her steam-wreathed profile to the fervid surface of a magic cauldron, and lifting one hand in delight at what she read there; and on the tea-pot she was Cleopatra, small breasts perfect as flower-buds beneath a simple robe, bare arms outstretched and the delicate triangle of a heel raised from the sole of a sandal as she stepped forward beseechingly to someone unseen.

"And the tea, also, that is very beautiful."

"Now," said Saphique, "you're being silly."

Sansiega looked towards her with an expression of mock seriousness, but saw again, through the triangle of Saphique's elbow as Saphique put down her tea-cup, what was stuck to the tea-pot. She tried to smother the laughter that rose at once in her throat with a sip of tea. And choked.

"See?" said Saphique, who had picked up three lumps of sugar.

"Yes, silly," admitted Sansiega, putting down her tea-cup and pulling a handkerchief from her jeans to wipe at her chin and lips.

"Throw?" asked Saphique.

Sansiega folded away the handkerchief.

"Throw," she said.

Saphique held a sugar lump up between the thumb and forefinger of her right hand. Sansiega watched it, her mouth half-open.

"Ready?"

"Ready."

Saphique's hand jerked, released, and the sugar lump flew across the table towards Sansiega, who darted her head for it, mouth opened wide, snapping shut.

"Missed," said Saphique. "One to me. Next one?"

"Next one."

From the slim fingers, the second sugar lump, spinning through the air towards her. Sansiega ducked in her chair, trying to take the lump on the rise, mouth opened wide again. She felt it strike her upper lip, almost painfully, and glance away to the floor.

"Nearly! Third?"

"Third," said Sansiega, and, rising in her chair, threw herself forward at the table for the third sugar lump, to catch it perfectly while it was still on the rise. She closed her mouth on the small hardness; crunched; began to suck.

"More good luck than judgement," said Saphique.

Sansiega rolled her eyes and twisted the lips of her closed, sucking mouth ironically.

"Now you have to say, 'Sugar sooth, sugar sooth, sugar sooth, sweets to the sweet'," said Saphique, "or it doesn't count."

Sansiega shook her head vigorously, crunched again, sucked, said through a still quarter-full mouth, "Not fair."

"Why not?"

Sansiega lifted her cup, drank deeply, and swirled tea around her mouth for a second before replying.

"Because you didn't say."

"I don't have to."

"Yes, you do."

"No, I don't."

"Yes, you *do*. Or it's cheating."

"OK, sugar, just this once, you win. More tea? Why are you laughing again?"

"I, I-yuh can't say."

"Why not?"

"You would kill me."

Saphique drained the tea in her cup and put it down in its saucer. She stood up and began to circle the table.

"OK, I'll kill you anyway. So you may as well tell me."

Sansiega put down her tea-cup, stood up, and began to circle the table away from Saphique.

"No, I still can't," she said.

They circled the table once. Saphique stopped and began to circle in the opposite direction. Stopped again. Circled back. Sansiega, too, stopped and began to circle in the opposite direction. Stopped again. Circled back. Like a mirror.

"Why not?" Saphique asked.

"You'd kill me more cruelly."

"*Now* I'm going to kill you cruelly. As cruelly as I can."

She lunged and Sansiega, with a squeak, bending her stomach in like a bow, just evaded the hooked, clutching fingers.

"But," said Saphique, "if you tell me, I will kill you quickly. You will feel nothing. I promise."

"No, I would rather die cruelly."

And suddenly, Sansiega's hand had dipped down into the sugar bowl, plucked up a handful of sugar lumps.

"Cruelly!" she shouted, and threw them at Saphique. Laughing, Saphique ducked, hands protecting her face, and Sansiega hurdled a corner of the table and ran for the door of the solarium.

"Cheat!" shouted Saphique, and began to run after her.

The floor shuddered with running feet.

A squeak.

The sound of two bodies falling.

"Got you!"

Sansiega squirmed beneath her lover. Luxuriously. Something caught in Saphique's throat. Her ears hummed with desire. She slid off. Caught Sansiega in her arms. Turned her roughly to her.

"Kiss?"

"Yes."

"...ngquestion?"

"Question?"

"Question."

"Ask me."

"Do you love me?"

"Love you?"

"Yes."

*"Hasta siempre."*

Then, after a pause:

"Your mouth tastes of sugar ... stop laughing!"

# Seventeen

Alanna said, "So this is the famous book."

She leant on one elbow, turning it over, examining it.

The cover was white. On the front there was a wood-cut in black of a palaeolithic stone figure, hugely breasted and buttocked; above, in red, the name of the book.

*BERRIA ATALANTEA.*

The cross-bars of the "A"'s were shaped like "v"'s, attached to uprights that didn't join at the top, supporting a straight top piece that overlapped them on either side.

She opened it and read, silently, *Gorbata eta mukizapi batzu ere erakuts iezazkidazu.*

She tried to read the line aloud, stumbled, started again, laughed.

"*Diana*, what a language!"

Sansiega said, "Yes, it's difficult."

Alanna turned the pages. On some pages, blocks of text had been marked out in transparent green marker pen, with annotations in the margin in neat, small pencil.

*Hamburgo, 1/X/91.*

*Niza, 23/VII/91.*

*Atenas, 11/XI/90.*

She stopped leafing and turned the pages back.

*Atenas, 11/XI/90.*

She had recognized a word in the marked section.

*Matricida.*

She sat up in the bed, marking the place with her finger.

"Isn't this a Spanish word?" she said.

Sansiega looked at the page.

"Yes. It is the name of a band. They are quite famous in Spain. They play necro-industrial *feminista*."

"What does the section say?"

"Let me have the book."

Alanna handed it to her.

Sansiega read for a few seconds, her lips moving silently.

"It says about how a man was killed. Then it says, 'When he was dead, the way that the blood was running from his mouth remembered her of a line from a song of *Matricida*.' Then it gives the line. It is a sort of poetry. It is difficult to traduce. More or less it says, 'All the rivers are dry, and only the sun is singing'."

"Does it talk about this sort of music a lot in the book?"

"Yes, of course. The woman who wrote it, she was a singer in a Basque band necro-industrial *feminista* called *Lamiak*."

Alanna looked at her, raising her eyebrows.

"We thought that the King liked that music, once," she said. "One of the first times he killed, someone was using a video-camera to film a wedding or something nearby. They also recorded the sound of a car stereo playing music very loudly. I can't remember what the name of the group was. Something medical. I think. Latin. Anyway, we thought maybe it was the King's car but in the end we couldn't prove it."

"Where was the killing?"

"Rome, in July last year."

Sansiega started flipping pages, stopped.

*"Roma."*

She read silently, then looked up.

"Was the band called *Infibulatrix?*"

"Yeah, that rings a bell."

"How did you find the name of the band?"

"We asked John Peel. He's a famous DJ who's interested in that sort of music. You know, a disk jockey, someone who plays records on the radio. We tried to contact the record company too, but they'd gone out of business."

"Not in Spain."

"What?"

"Not in Spain. They still exist in Spain. One of my friends in Bilbao, she works in a record shop. They do business for the record company there."

*"Jesa Christina."*

"I think they changed their name, but they still exist. Something else too. Some of *Infibulatrix*'s records, they are only available through the mail. Maybe, if the record was one of those, you can find his address. Do you remember what the song was?"

"No. At the time we didn't follow up the point very hard. We thought it was probably just a coincidence, and didn't have the time to follow up every tiny lead. But if you're right, well, it could be the best one we've ever had."

"Can you let me hear the recording?"

"I can, yeah. Come on, get dressed. I'll take you to listen to it."

# Eighteen

"And he's coming? They've no way of stopping him?"

"None. He's ours now, as long as we want him."

"OK. Good. What are we going to do when the shit hits the fan?"

"The French, you mean?"

"The French, the Germans, the Italians, the whole fucking set, except perhaps the Dutch."

"Sit tight. It's not going to be easy but there's nothing they'll be able to do. Openly."

"OK. One other thing though. I want that bitch at the Met off the job ASAP. See to it, will you?"

"Sure. Does this mean we're going to release the proof to the *Times*?"

"Not yet. We're not quite ready to do that yet. Ideally, we should give everything another week or two, but she's just too dangerous to leave in place as it is."

# Nineteen

"*¿Hola? Soy Sansiega. ¿Está María-José? ¿Sí? ... Gracías.*"
She made a thumbs-up to Alanna.
They were in Alanna's office. Sansiega was sitting on a corner of the desk, propping the handset of the phone under one ear with her shoulder. Next to her, a tape-recorder was set up. Alanna was sitting behind the desk. They had played the tape that had been taken from the wedding video; Sansiega had recognized the music as coming from *Infibulatrix*'s "Click-Clack-Clunk" album. It had been banned from public sale in America because of the cover art; in Europe, the recording company, Femme Neck, had sold it only through mail order.
Which meant, maybe...
"*¡Hola! María, ¿qué tal?* ... *bien, muy bien.* Listen, do you still work in that record shop *en el Casco?* Yeah? Good. Listen, you do mail order for Femme Neck there, don't you? ... yeah, OK. Look, I'm gonna ask you to do something for me, maybe you won't like it, but *hombre*, look, I wouldn't ask if it weren't real important. *Mas que la hostia* ... OK, listen. You keep the addresses of people who have ordered stuff by mail there, don't you? For lists and stuff, yeah? ... OK, look, I know. But it's real important. I wouldn't ask otherwise, you know? ... OK, OK. Listen, what I want you to do is to find the names of everyone who ordered the "Click, Clack, Clunk" of *Infibulatrix*. Cleek, Clack, Cloonk. You want me to spell it? OK."
She spelt the name of the album.
"OK? You'll do that? ... *María, te quiero. Eres corazón de mi corazón.* When can you get back to me? ... OK, right. You can fax it from the shop? *Bueno. Buenísimo.* Hold a moment, will you?"
She cupped her hand over the mouthpiece of the phone and spoke to Alanna.
"What is your fax number?"
Alanna pulled out a draw in her desk, pulled out a pad and pen, wrote, and pushed the pad across the table to Sansiega.
"*Gracías* ... María, this is it."
She gave the number, thanked her friend again and put the phone down.
"Did you understand?"
"A little. She's going to fax the names of all the people who ordered the

88

album, right?"

"Yes. She's going round to the record shop where she works now. She has the keys. She says it'll take about half-an-hour. She'll be in big trouble if her boss finds out, though. Where is the fax machine?"

"I'll take you to it. Come on, we'll pick up a coffee on the way. Have you got a fifty-pee piece?"

The phone began to ring.

Alanna raised her eyebrows and picked it up.

"Hello, Alanna Kirk ... yes, sir, I'm working on it now. There's a new lead ... what? ... right ... right ... OK, thank you. Thank you. Goodbye." She put the phone down, hard. Her lips had gone pale, and quivered faintly.

"What's wrong?"

"I've been suspended. They tried to ring me at home, tried here when I wasn't there. I've been fucking-well suspended. Pending an investigation into the allegations of a conspiracy between the Slaughter King and members of the investigation team. Meaning, me. Fuck, he threatened to do it, but I never thought it would be so quick."

"Who threatened you? Threatened you what?"

Alanna's eyes focused on her. The pale lips twisted, trying to smile.

"Doesn't matter. Come on, let's get that coffee and go and wait for the fax. Fuck 'em. Fuck 'em all to hell."

The fax machine was in a downstairs office. They sat on the desk next to it, sipping their coffee.

Alanna said, her eyes unfocused again with anger, "What if he didn't order it in Spain?"

"It should be OK. Everything's on computer, I think she'll be able to get details of people from countries beside Spain. Anyway, Femme Neck in Bilbao sell records to France, Italy, Germany. If he bought the record, his name should be on the computer."

"If."

"If. It's the best chance you have though, isn't it?"

"Yes, it's the best chance. And I'm suspended."

The fax machine beeped. Paper started to emerge from it. They watched it eagerly. The paper dropped into the basket beneath the machine. Sansiega snatched it up and smoothed it out on the desk. Another page started to emerge from the fax.

Alanna looked at the list of names and addresses, which looked as though they had been run off on a computer printer. Twenty or so of them. Underneath the list something was scrawled in Spanish.

"What does it say at the bottom?"

"It says that these are all the names for Spain. Germany, Italy, France follow."

"*Christina*, there'll be hundreds."

Sansiega was running her finger down the list. Alanna reached into the basket as the next sheet dropped from the fax.

Sansiega said, "No, no. Look, I think this might be the one."

Alanna dropped the sheet back into the basket and turned.

"Where?"

"Look, here."

Alanna read the name.

*Patricia Huercos, Flat 3, Esc. Der., 11 Vía Central, Baracaldo, Vizcaya.*

"Yeah, what about it?"

"Baracaldo is a small town. It's near Bilbao, on the river. Don't you remember, one of the killings was there. Two years ago."

"Yes, I think I remember. I remember it was near Bilbao, anyway."

"And there's something else, too."

"What?"

"The name. Patricia Huercos."

"Patricia is a woman's name."

"I know. Only women can buy *Infibulatrix* records. But listen. Patricia Huercos. Señora P Huercos. Señora Puercos. In Spanish, *puerco* means pig. Male pig."

"It might be a joke. It might be someone's nickname."

"Nickname?"

"Yeah, nickname. It means someone's joke name. Like, you know, that footballer, Spanish footballer. What's his name? *Butragueno* or something. You know, the vulture. That's his nickname."

"Oh, I understand. *El buitro*. The vulture. Nickname. Do you like football?"

"No, I hate it. I had a girlfriend once, years ago. Football fan. You know how it is."

They looked at each other.

Sansiega said, "Yes, I know how."

They both laughed.

Alanna said, "Look, I don't trust this. It's too easy. But if this is him, I have to get there at once."

"You? Why don't you tell the police?"

90

"I am the police, remember? Even when I'm suspended. I can't tell you why I can't tell my superiors. I just have to stop him. Kill him. I shouldn't even tell you this, but he's going to come to this country. Soon."

"How do you know?"

Alanna looked at her.

"I can't tell you. It's better for you not to know. I just have to get there to stop him, if he's still there."

"If so, then I have to come with you."

"No, it's too dangerous."

"Do you speak Spanish?"

"A little."

"Do you know the Basque country?"

"No."

"So, I have to come with you."

"No."

"Yes. It's necessary. If you go alone, it will be inefficient. You will waste time. You might miss him. A hundred things. If you want to catch him, I have to go with you."

Another page fell into the basket from the fax.

"OK, OK, you win. You can come with me. Let's get rid of these other pages. Have you got your cigarette lighter?"

# *Twenty*

Saphique was drunk, just a little, and glad to be so, for she had grown bored in the hours by herself in the house, and lonely.

And yet, not lonely, for she could have had company any time she chose, on the phone or minutes away by taxi at the home of a friend. But the only company she desired was not available to her.

Ten minutes before, the phone had rung.

"Hello?"

"Hello, Saphique? It's me, Sansiega."

"Sansiega, where are you? You said you would only be two or three hours! I've been worried sick."

"Saphique, I'm sorry. I called home this morning, when you were out. One of my sisters, she's very ill. I have to go home, at once."

"Have you got enough money for it?"

"No, but it's OK, my family, they're buying me a plane ticket in Bilbao, you know? Through the phone. It will be OK."

"Will you be coming here, to say goodbye?"

"No, Saphique, I've got everything I need. I'm sorry. Really really sorry. I can't. Now I'm at the airport. The flight is very soon. I will call you when I am in Spain. I'm sorry."

"Me too. I hope your sister gets better quickly. *Te quiero.*"

"*Gracías. Te quiero a ti. Muchísimo. Adios.* See you."

"See you."

And the connection had broken, but it had taken her a minute, nearly, to put the phone down.

Now, she sat on the carpet and exercised, slowly, with the sweet acid ache of muscles and tendons stretched and held to their full through carefully counted seconds serving to distract her mind from the Sansiega-less days that stretched ahead.

A tall glass of wine stood on the carpet beside her, set wide against an accidental upset, and as she finished each *asana* she stretched for it and took it up and sipped from it, washing out her mouth with the sharp, cold taste of the wine.

Suddenly, she felt the need of music and hopped herself forward halfway through a back-strengthening exercise to the alcove of the producer's stereo, the shelves of the CD collection. Some of them were hers, from when they'd been lovers. Her hand played over the narrow faces of the CDs, awaiting her decision.

She chose, and slid back to complete the back-strengthening exercise. It was half-way through an *asana* particularly good for the popliteal muscles that she was reminded of the tea-set still sitting in the solarium from the day before. She had forgotten to clear it away. Sansiega had too. She smiled, remembering.

She completed the *asana* and sat up.

She had had enough.

"Lazy-bones," she said to herself.

Not guilty.

I'll clear away the tea things as soon as I've had a shower.

Promise.

On the stereo the album's title track began.

It had been used for the video in which Saphique had starred as Medea. "The Witch".

She stood up suddenly.

No, I'll have a cup first.

She turned up the volume on the stereo so that she could hear it in the shower if she left the door of the ground floor bathroom open. Returning in a kimono of grey silk, she felt relaxed, clean, a little sleepy. She turned down the stereo and went into the kitchen for a tray.

In the solarium, she put the tray down and started to lift the tea things onto it.

Suddenly, she stopped, staring at the tea-pot.

She sat down and lifted it.

Turned it into the light.

The design on the pot had been altered.

How in heaven?

A later scene from the video.

The death-scene, with the asp hanging coiled from its teeth in her breast. But no, no, the rest of the design was identical — the bare, outstretched arms, raised heel, sidebent, beseeching head — and the asp was of pale gold.

And the asp was no asp.

She put the pot down heavily, splashing cold tea on her hand. She didn't feel it.

A hair.

A blonde hair.

A blonde pubic hair.

Her stomach tightened and she felt her throat grow narrow and cold. For a moment she thought she would be unable to breathe; the sob, when it came, was half relief. Half. The next, not so. Wholly agony of mind. The hair, forgotten. The unfamiliarity of the emotion that bloomed within her brain acted to sharpen her anguish. A faint aftertaste of wine in her mouth was suddenly sour and strong and a dozen minor pains and aches and not-quite-as-should-be-so's within her body ran and sharpened like stars glimpsed again after blinked-away tears.

And then everything grew dull and her guts, all her being, seemed to lurch up inside her, opening her throat, her mouth as though she were a puppet, and she wailed for the loss of her trust in her love, for the fear, the terror, the horror of the thought that maybe the love of the love was lost too. This was the dread thought that seemed to shrivel her with extreme cold, as though she were a flower in frost.

Some time later she became aware that she had been dropping sugar lumps into cup half-full of cold tea — one was poised ready in her fingers. She dropped it back into the sugar bowl.

How long she had been adding the lumps she was not sure.

She lifted the cup and saw that the tea within it was thick and slow with sugar. She turned the cup and watched the tea move sluggishly. Her face was faintly visible on its surface. She held the cup away from her, over the floor and tipped it. She thought the pouring tea sounded like blood. Thick.

Drops of it splattered her bare ankle.

Cold, thick blood.

She dropped the cup and stood up, looking out through the glass wall of the solarium to the garden.

As she looked the sun emerged from behind the clouds: for an instant, everywhere, the garden blazed, green or vividly coloured, stretching wide to left and right and far in front of her; and then the sun was shrouded again.

She smiled sardonically.

A fragment of china cut into the sole of her right foot as she left the solarium and the foot began to bleed, leaving bloody marks behind as she walked to the bedroom. The first few were small, irregularly shaped, but after that they captured the outline of her sole and toes almost fully, bloody marks of a single foot against the carpet like the symbolry for a dualist goddess of suffering and oblivion.

# Twenty-One

Sansiega put the phone down, paused a moment to let an old woman trundle her wheeled suitcase past the booth, and walked over to Alanna.
Alanna said, "Do you think she believed you?"
Sansiega shouldered her bag. The public address system started to announce the departure of a flight to Malaysia.
"Of course. With me, she's thick."
"What a conceited little bitch you are."
"Me? Fuck you then. *Puerca.*"
"I understood that."
*"Me importa un bledo.* Where can we get a coffee?"
Alanna looked at her watch.
"Ee lass, I dunno. I dunno. Mebbe thee and me's just time fra quick un."
"Speak English."
The flight left almost exactly on time. They had three seats to themselves. Sansiega sat by the window. As they lifted off, the air was very clear, but a few seconds later the window went opaque with white cloud. When, just as suddenly, the air was clear again, they were very high, and the patches of earth visible through breaks in the cloud below where like a thin, vivid crust, marked with the thin threads of roads along which, just at the limit of vision, tiny multi-coloured crumbs were crawling.
Far away to the north, hanging against a white bank of cloud like a jewel on snow, Sansiega could see a balloon. As she watched it, the plane began to turn; just before the balloon slid from view, she saw a hairlike spark of flame appear beneath it.
Alanna was saying something to her.
"Sorry?"
"I was saying, do they serve a meal on the flight?"
"Yeah, I think so. It'll be pretty crap. If we had time, I could take you to eat some very good food in the *País Basque. Euskadi.* It's said the Basques have the best of the French food and the Spanish. The best in the world."
"Maybe we will have time."
When the meal trolleys came round, they were flying over the Bay of Biscay. The sea was very blue, wrinkled minutely with waves. The food

95

wasn't as bad as Sansiega had predicted. Not quite.

When the trays were taken away Sansiega started to read the Spanish newspaper she had bought at the beginning of the flight.

"Anything interesting happened since you went away?"

"No, it looks not. There is an article on the King. You see?"

She held the newspaper open.

## ¿EL REVENIMIENTO DEL «REY» A ESPAÑA?

"Yeah. What does the article say?"

"It says that he perhaps will be starting to kill a lot again in Spain. There is also something about the *pression* on you. The pressure. The journalist does not think it is a good thing."

"Glad to hear it."

"He says ... wait, look. That is the *País Basque*. The Basque Country."

She put the newspaper down. A streak of coastline had appeared along the horizon. Below, the wave-wrinkles were becoming flecked with white.

Alanna asked, "How long until we land?"

"Oh, half-an-hour, maybe. Maybe less."

The plane began to lose height and the coastline grew nearer, rising into tiny cliffs and coves, with a thin yellow rind of beach. A boat, small as a seed, lay black against the purple-blue sea.

They passed from sea to land, banking, still losing height. The sun was shining and the earth below them seemed very green. A grey rope of river wound beneath them. They were low enough to see cars and houses clearly, and they were still dropping, still turning. Sunlight burst minutely off the windows of cars beneath them. The plane rocked slightly, flew smoothly for a few seconds, rocked again, harder.

They were very low now. A loop of river appeared beneath the window, and Sansiega could see water-weeds swaying in the current in the shallow water along the bank. A house slid by, big as a head, many-eyed.

The plane rocked again.

Looking along the plane to the wing, she could see the control surfaces judder.

"What is that?"

She looked sideways at Alanna.

"The wind. It's very strong near the sea."

"Earth-Mother preserve us."

"Don't worry. *No seas cobarde.* Don't be a coward. Ow!"

The plane's height held steady now. They rushed in over the earth, the river sliding in and out of view beneath them. A tone sounded on the public address system and the *NO SMOKING/NO FUMAR* lights came on. One of the stewardesses started to speak in Spanish. As she finished and started again in English, the *FASTEN SEATBELTS/ABROCHENSE CINTURONES* lights came on.

They fastened their seatbelts. A patch of thin mist whipped past the window. The plane was rocking almost continuously now.

Without knowing why, Sansiega was suddenly frightened. It wasn't the plane, or the landing. Not the fact of the landing. Its symbolism. She glanced sideways at Alanna, who smiled at her. She looked away, at the window. The airport was ahead of them. A long arm of runway swung toward them. Further away, beyond the airport buildings, cars streamed on a four-lane motorway. She stared at them, trying to read something in their colours and shapes.

The plane had stopped shaking. They were seconds away from landing. Grass and concrete were blurred into streaming green and gray by their speed. She held her breath. Something thumped at the underside of the plane, thumped again, and the runway was roaring beneath them, buzzing in the seats.

*"Bienvenidos al País Vasco,"* Sansiega said.

*"Muchísimas* thanks."

The plane began to slow. The stewardess started speaking again.

They walked across the tarmac towards the reception building. The sun was shining but the air was thin and cold. A wind swung across them. They walked faster. Neither of them had much luggage, only what they could carry with them onto the plane: Alanna, a black shoulder bag, Sansiega a plastic carrier from an independent food co-op in London (a tall, long-haired woman in Lord Kitchener pose; *"The Goddess Wants You ... To Save the Earth"*).

Ahead of the them, the line of passengers began to slow as passports were examined by a man in uniform inside a glass booth marked *PASAPORTEAK/PASAPORTES.*

Alanna asked, "Will we be able to hire a car quickly?"

"Yes. No problem."

They pushed their passports under the glass grill. The man glanced at them and pushed them back, looking bored. They walked inside the building. People were standing by the luggage conveyor, waiting for their suitcases and bags to swing into view from beneath the strips of black rubber at one end.

They hired a Fiat. It smelt of cigarette smoke and too much sun. As Sansiega accelerated away from the rental garage, along the line of taxis waiting beside the terminal exit, Alanna wound the window down. Her hair danced in the cold wind. As they approached the turn-off for the motorway she had seen from the plane, Sansiega pushed a button on the car stereo.

A man's voice filled the car. Sansiega turned the volume down, braking and looking left and right for a break in the stream of cars.

She pulled out fast. A horn blared behind them. She smiled and looked up into the mirror, sticking her tongue out. On the stereo, the man had stopped speaking and was being applauded. The applause cut off and a newsreader's began speaking, quickly.

"Who was that?" Alanna asked.

"Manuel Fraga. He's a politician. Making some speech about immigration, I think. Find another station, if you want."

"No, it's OK."

She wound the window back up, leaving a small gap at the top.

"Better," she said. "How long before we're there?"

"Depends of the circulation. I would say, half an hour."

Alanna was silent for a moment.

She said, "I would feel better with a gun."

Sansiega glanced at her.

"It's possible to get one, but it would take a long time. But if you want..."

"No. Time is more important. We have to stop him. If we can. If it's his house. *If.*"

Sansiega lifted her hand and ran it over her head. She muttered something.

"What?"

She glanced in the wing mirror and overtook a van before replying. *FRANCISCOS DE BURGOS.*

"My hair. I need to cut it. To have it cut."

Alanna laughed.

A sign loomed up on the corner of the road and cracked past. On the horizon ahead, a line of grey had appeared. Blue-grey. The sun was still shining but the air coming through the window was very cold. Alanna shivered a little and wound the window all the way back up. On the stereo the news had finished and music was playing, Euro-pop, jangly guitar with Spanish lyrics.

Alanna said, "Have you got a tape?"

"Yeah. In the pocket of my jacket."

Alanna leaned over to the backseat, where Sansiega had thrown the jacket when they got into the car. She felt the right pocket, then the left, and drew out a cassette.

*Episiotomy.*

*"El Cuchillo Siempre Tiene Razón".*

A sickly yellow cover with a medical instrument on it, outlined in red, that looked like a cross between a scapel and a pair of scissors.

She shelled the tape and pushed it into the stereo.

"How boringly mainstream your tastes in music are," she said.

Sansiega looked at her, half-smiling, not having quite understood.

*"No sé,"* she said, looking back at the road. "Oh, I remember something now. In your flat, have you found a tape of *Dysmenorrhoea*?"

The stereo crashed with static, spiked through with the sharp soprano belches of what sounded like a cross between a drum machine and a performing seal.

"No. Why? What was it called?"

"'Tit for Tat'. I've lost it. Can't remember where."

The lead singer started in.

Alanna said, "No, I haven't seen it. There was a tape behind the back of the sofa, remember? Was that it?"

"No. It doesn't matter. It will be found or it won't."

"Very true. And you probably stole it in the first place anyway."

"How can you think that?"

She laughed. The line of grey had grown and come closer. It was the sea. No, not the sea. The mouth of a river. Even at a distance the water looked dirty. As they got closer Alanna could see the river water fanning out into the sea, dirty grey against dirty blue. Further out, silhouetted darkly against the bright sky, there were wind-surfers.

Sansiega turned off from the motorway, heading toward the river. The fields and occasional houses between which they had been travelling were replaced abruptly by suburbia. The houses were big, most of them standing in their own gardens. They looked expensive.

Sansiega said, "This is where the rich buggers live."

"You took the words right out of my mouth."

Sansiega turned again.

"I'm going to park," she said.

"Where is the *Vía Central*?"

*"Thentral."*

"Fuck off. *Thentral.*"

"It's on the other side of the river. There's a bridge. A special kind of bridge. I hate taking cars on it."

"OK. You're the boss. Where are you going to park?"

"Here."

She pulled into the kerb, half in the shadow of a huge tree, covered in small white flowers, that hung over a high brick wall.

They got out. The road and pavement were covered with fallen flowers from the tree. Already, one was resting on the roof of the car, lying small and perfect against the dull red paint.

"It's safe?"

"Here? What is it you say in English? Safe as a house?"

"Safe as houses."

"As houses. This way."

She began to walk in the direction Alanna had last seen the river. Alanna ran a pace to catch up.

Sansiega said, "I want to buy a knife. Two knives. One for you, one for me. OK?"

"Yeah, OK."

"I think that it's better for you to buy them. They will remember me more easily. If anything goes wrong."

"I don't speak Spanish."

"You do. Enough. I'll tell you what to say. Anyway, there are lots of tourists in the *País Basque.*"

"And not many skinhead dykes?"

Sansiega snorted.

"No. Not enough. Look, there's the bridge."

The river had appeared in front of them again, wide and grey. There was also a bridge. As Sansiega had said, a special kind of bridge: two tall, rusting metal towers on either bank with a complicated network of cables linking them from which hung, moving slowly toward the opposite bank, a huge metal shoebox. With windows.

"What do you call that in English?"

"*Sophia* knows. A carbuncle, probably."

The vague shapes of people and cars could be seen through the windows. The giant box was shaking faintly. They walked up to the base of the tower on their side of the bank and bought tickets from an automatic ticket machine set into one of the pillars. Old people were sitting on benches facing the river, waiting, apparently, for the shoebox to return. It was nearly at the other side now.

100

"How long does it take it get back?"

"Depends of how many people are waiting. Fag?"

"Yeah, go on. *Carpe diem*. I may as well enjoy myself before I catch something fatal from being near that river."

Sansiega handed her a cigarette.

They sat on a metal beam and stared at the river.

"Ta."

Close to, the water looked worse. It was a deep, dirty grey, its surface twisted with sluggish eddies. It stank.

The box had stopped on the other side of the river and little streams of people were running from it on either side. A seagull swooped low over the water in mid-river, its reflection faint, dull white in the water's surface. They waited.

The cables above their heads hummed and the metal beam vibrated faintly beneath them. The box was on its way back. More people had bought tickets. Three young men in shiny leather jackets and tight faded jeans stood hopping against the cold and kicking small stones into the river. One had glanced at them for a second.

The box was in mid-river, swaying. Sansiega threw her cigarette onto the concrete and stood up. The old people had got off the benches and started to gather near where the box would make its landing. The three young men were laughing at something, not kicking at stones now, just bouncing on the spot, watching the box come in.

Alanna stood up as well, dropping her cigarette to the ground and standing on it. She walked after Sansiega. In one end of the box was a huge pair of doors. As it slid in over the bank and stopped, the doors opened and a ramp was run out and down onto the concrete by a pair of attendants in blue uniforms. Alanna could see inside the box now. It was hollow, just a long space divided with railings into a long central space for cars, and two narrower spaces on either side for pedestrians. Cars and people started to come out of the box. The air misted greyly with exhaust.

They got on, walking to the far end. There were no seats; they leaned against the railing, watching cars bump up the ramp and drive inside. After five minutes, the doors were closed again and the box set off to the opposite bank. Beyond the windows, the river flowed slowly.

They reached the opposite bank and got off. There was a hillside in front of them, terraced with houses. Sansiega nodded forward at a steep concrete stairway and they set off up it. It was divided in two by metal railings, cankered thickly with rust. By the time they reached the top, their palms were red.

Sansiega turned left, up a tree-lined avenue. They crossed the avenue, walked down a narrow alley dotted with occasional dog turds and were on a street lined with shops and cafes.

They crossed the avenue and stopped in front of a shop marked *FERRETERIA*. In the window there were electric kettles and irons, brooms, dustpans, a sleek vacuum cleaner, portable TVs.

Sansiega asked, "You OK then?"

Alanna walked into the shop.

After a couple of minutes she came out again, smiling and carrying a paper bag. She held the top of the bag open. A set of kitchen knives sealed with plastic onto a cardboard base.

"Good," said Sansiega. "Now, Flat 3."

*Vía Central* was a short, narrow street down near the sea-front. The buildings were old, built of wood and grey-brown stone, five and six storeys high. Cars were parked on both sides of it, leaving barely enough space down the middle for one-way traffic. There was a small supermarket on the corner and a Chinese restaurant and a couple of bars further along it.

Number 11 was next to one of the bars. There was a solid, battered-looking set of doors and an intercom in the wall next to them. Most of the flat numbers had a name next to them, but FLAT 3 said only that, in neat black pen.

Sansiega tested the doors. They were locked.

"*Vale*. Listen," she said.

She explained what she wanted Alanna to do, then walked down to the supermarket with a 500-*peseta* coin. When she walked back with a plastic bag full of shopping, Alanna was sitting in the bar on the opposite side of the road, watching the street. Sansiega walked into the bar next to the flats, propped up her shopping against the footrest and ordered a *zurito*. She sat sipping it, glancing across to Alanna occasionally.

Apart from Sansiega, the bar was empty. After serving her, the bar-owner lifted a section of the bar and came out to sweep up the debris of lunch. He was old and overweight and moved slowly. His breath whistled as he guided the toothpicks and the crumpled paper napkins into a pile. The television was on, showing cartoons.

On the other side of the street, Alanna watched the entrance to number 11. Two people had come out of it almost as soon as she started watching, two teenagers carrying folders and schoolbags. After that, nothing.

Quarter of an hour passed. An old woman came through the doors with a string bag. She walked slowly up the street towards the supermarket. Ten minutes later, the string bag half-full, she appeared again, walking back.

Alanna stood up and stepped out into the street, lifting a hand. Sansiega drained her third *zurito*, dropped something onto the top of the bar and stooped for her shopping. The old woman was about to come level with the doors. Alanna dropped her hand and Sansiega stepped out from the bar, carrying the shopping in both hands.

Alanna turned and went back into the bar. The owner was standing at the end nearest the street, watching her as though he thought she was going to walk off without paying.

"*¿Cuántas?*"

"*Trescientas cuarenta.*"

She paid and left the bar. A car was driving slowly up the street. She stepped between two parked cars and let it go by before walking across. The old woman and Sansiega had gone, but there was a crack of shadow showing between the doors.

As she stepped up to the doors they swung open.

She walked inside.

"Did it!"

Sansiega was smiling. She had propped the shopping up against the wall of the short corridor that ran forward to the first flight of stairs. Light was shining from higher up the stairs, but near the doors it was very dark.

"Was the old lady not suspicious?"

"No. I don't think she really noticed me."

# Twenty-Two

He hadn't killed on the ferry. Of course, there'd been opportunity to, plenty of it in the darkness of the night crossing, but She had warned him against it as he had knelt before Her.

Too risky.

He understood.

He hadn't liked to leave the car. Without it, he felt weak, like an insect with its exoskeleton cut away or a snake just after moulting. No, not weak. Weaker. Less strong. Less strong.

He'd sat among the rows of seats towards the bow and allowed himself to fall half-submerged in sleep, dreaming and knowing he dreamed. He heard Her speaking to him again in the mutter of the engines; at the beginning of the crossing, as he'd leaned on the railings at the stern and watched the light-jewelled land slip away, he'd heard Her voice in the sea and wind.

Now, he was arrived.

He drove his car from the guts of the ferry, a feverish metal parasite disgorged onto a fat green carcass. Customs was no problem. He had hardly any luggage and he'd dressed as She'd advised him, not too rich-looking, not too poor. He said little, just smiled a lot. The customs officials thought he was stupid, but he didn't push the act too far.

As he drove away from the ferry terminus he wound down the window and spat out into the lightening air.

He drove quickly, eager to begin, following the A164 north towards York. The air grew lighter. It was drizzling. The windscreen wipers sang to him.

He was driving through farmland, green fields, low stone walls, hedges. Here and there he passed what looked in the dim light like snow-drifts along the hedges or around trees: sheep huddled together for shelter against the rain.

He watched expectantly.

After ten minutes or so, in one field, he saw a smaller patch of white a long way from shelter. He braked carefully, stopping the car well to the side of the road, and got out. He opened the boot and took out a coil of rope.

The top of the stone wall was slicked with wet lichen. He climbed onto it carefully and jumped off into the field. His feet splashed loudly in a thin layer of liquid mud beneath the grass; his trousers were splattered with the stuff, brown against black, like constellations of shit auguring victory.

The drizzle swirled around him, wetting his face and hands.

He walked across the field towards the patch of white.

As he had hoped, it was a sheep, a sick sheep, lying on its side. Its chest rose and fell rapidly and its muzzle was streaked with yellowish foam. As he got near to it, it tried to get to its feet and run off, but it staggered and fell over almost at once.

He gripped it by the back of the head, winding his fingers tightly into the wool. It bleated thinly and coughed.

He lashed the rope around its neck and forelimbs, finding it hard not laugh as the sheep coughed and wheezed like an old man. When he had finished he began to drag the sheep across the field towards the wall, one-handed, lifting it free of the ground for seconds at a time. It bleated and kicked its hindlimbs. The foam around its muzzle splashed against his hand, made watery by the rain.

He reached the wall and let go of the sheep. He stood resting his hands on his knees, panting. The sheep struggled on the ground. Mud sprayed against him. He kicked it in the ribs and stooped to get both hands on the rope around its neck, careful to keep clear of the sharp little hooves of the jerking hindlimbs.

After he'd hoisted it to the top of the wall and pushed it over, he thought he'd broken its neck. It was quite a drop on the other side, and after the heavy soft thump of landing, there wasn't any sound. He climbed over after it. It was sprawled along the roadside, head half-caught under the lashed-together forelimbs. He bent over it and laid a palm along its neck. It was still alive. It shivered. As he touched it, its eyes rolled in its head and its muzzle gaped, the two halves sewn together with strings of foam. Its teeth looked huge, blunt and heavy and yellow. Its tongue trembled soundlessly.

He lifted it up and dragged it to the back of the car. It could stand, balancing awkwardly on the single limb his rope had made of its forelimbs. He tied the free end of the road to the towbar of his car. The rope tautened as the sheep tugged at it, moving to one side and the other, pogo'ing awkwardly on its forelimbs.

Apart from the thick wheeze of its breathing, it made no sound. There were about two metres of free rope. He'd probably be able to see the sheep in his rear-view mirror. He ran his eyes over the knots again and slapped the sheep with ironic camaraderie over the back. His hand thudded solidly on the damp wool.

He glanced up and down the road, and walked round the car to the driver's door. He opened it and got in, looking in the mirror.

No.

He adjusted it.

No.

*Así es la vida.*

He started the engine and drove off, slowly, keeping at about five kilometres an hour.

After a kilometre, he decided it was time, and stood slowly on the accelerator. Still nothing in the mirror, but at around fifteen kilometres an hour the car began to vibrate faintly and grew sluggish to respond to the steering wheel.

His penis bulged, stiff as the gearstick.

He drove for another three kilometres and then stopped.

It was getting too light, and besides, much further and there wouldn't be much left.

He got out and walked to the back of the car. A broad wavering strip of red stretched out down the road. The carcass was half worn away, white ground bone and friction-striped muscle showing everywhere through the torn wool. The hind limbs were nearly gone and the contents of the gut hung moist and frayed through the ground away lower ribs. The head was still mostly intact, but the shoulder-joints had been worn through completely, and the forelimbs were bound to the body now only by the ropes. Blood ran everywhere.

There was a stink of wet wool and dung.

He untied the rope and rolled the carcass to the side of the road with his feet, blood and rain remoistening the mud on his trousers.

He squatted beside it, unzipping his trousers. The rain felt icy on his glans penis for a moment. He thrust into the hot tattered guts, gripping the carcass by the head and neck to steady it against his rhythm. A second before orgasm, adding onanism to the sin of his necrozoophilia, he withdrew and watched his semen squirting white white white in the rain, mixing with the blood and water running off the carcass.

He tore up a handful of grass, wiped his glans and penis clean and stood up, zipping his trousers.

A good start.

He drove away.

Five minutes later it was light enough to switch the headlights off.

106

# Twenty-Three

Saphique groaned and opened her eyes.
The sunlight pouring into the room between a crack in the curtains was like the pubic hair of a Goddess.
Marilyn Monroe, apotheasized.
But she was a bottle-blonde.
Zeus, descending in a shower of piss.
Golden showers.
Golden hair.
Sansiega's mouth, clamped to a golden pubis.
Red tongue.
Moaning.
Cunt-sucking.
Her head ached.
She sat up.
There was an half-empty bottle of vodka on the floor, fallen over, with a damp patch underneath the neck of the bottle.
*Christina.*
She walked slowly to the bathroom and vomited copiously into the wide mouth of the lavatory.
Pressed the handle.
*Christina.*
I feel like shit.
I am shit.
She dressed in a sari of black silk and walked through to the living room with a packet of cigarettes and a lighter.
Sipping a fizzing glass of water, she started to set up the computer Goddess chess. It was the very latest thing in the rich pagan community in the States, her friend had said. Try it out. Might help you stop feeling depressed.
Saphique's fingers trembled. The pieces felt very smooth as she unpacked them and set them up on the board.
When the chess was set up she sat and stared at it.
It was shaped like a flower — an opened, three-petalled lotus whose heart was the playing board, a tessellation of triangles, green, white and red, that itself formed a triangle along whose sides the pieces were

arrayed in their double rows: green, white and red: jade, marble and ruby: thumb-high carved figures of delicate, incredible intricacy:—

in jade: a queen and daughter clothed in their own flowing hair, former with hands cupped and full of seeds, latter tipping a heavy amphora from whose mouth water was just beginning to spill, each flanked by a high priestess crowned with buds, arms and legs turned and lifted in dance, who is flanked in her turn by a swan grave and stately as the pleasure barge of a dowager-empress: at each end of the row, a dolphin, leaping; and in front of this row, a row of eight she-gazelles, small-horned and with bellies just swollen into pregnancy, and each in an individual attitude of grazing or rest, bestartlement or motion.

In marble: a queen and daughter clothed and coronated in garlands of flowers, former hefting a cornucopia spilling over with cereals and fruit, latter holding — her right hand — a wide bowl heaped with apples, and — in her left — a single apple, offered smilingly forward; each was flanked by a high priestess crowned with flowers, arms and lips lifted in benediction, who is flanked in her turn by an eagle crouched for flight: at each end of the row, a she-elephant and calf on a common base, suckled and suckling; and in front of this row, a row of eight she-leopards, ocellated cunningly with inlays of just barely lighter and darker marbles, and each in an individual attitude of watchfulness or indolence, minacity or playfulness.

In ruby: a queen and daughter strapped in armour and helm, former with hips triple-bound in a rope of skulls, animal and human, and swinging left-handed a notched and moon-curved sword, latter squeezing blood from a human heart in her right hand and gripping in her left a dripping sickle; each was flanked by a high priestess crowned with thorns and unwinding from her waist a noosed and heavy rope, who is flanked in her turn by a vulture lifting wings for flight: at each end of the row, a she-python coiled into a pyramid at whose apex the heavy, sagittate head bears unblinking crystal eyes; and in front of this row, a row of eight she-jackals, stark-ribbed and manged, and each in an individual attitude of caution or guardianship, attack or flight, or bearing in her jaws a bone or chunk of rotten flesh.

She picked up the computer and started to program it for solo-play.

It asked her for names for her two opponents.

Jade as Sansiega, ruby as Hel.

She picked up a leopard, moved it forward, placed it down, punched the move into the computer.

The LCD screen came up with Sansiega's move.

108

Queen's gazelle to queen's high priestess two.

She leaned across the board for a gazelle, lifted it, set it down.

Hel's move.

Queen's vulture's jackal to vulture's three.

She moved the piece; pondered the board a moment; lifted and set down an eagle.

Sansiega's move.

Daughter's swan's gazelle to swan's two; and, Hel, Queen's jackal to queen's high priestess three.

She moved the pieces. Cracked open the seal on the packet of cigarettes and lit one.

Put down down the second eagle.

Drew on the cigarette

Sansiega.

Queen's high priestess two gazelle to queen's high priestess three.

Hel.

Daughter's vulture to daughter's python two.

Already, the web of possibilities was thick. Her mind wandered amidst it. She moved the computer's pieces, pondered, picked up a leopard, placed it down. The LCD screen gave Sansiega's and Hel's moves; she moved the pieces, drew on the cigarette, stared down onto the board.

After a minute jade lost to ruby, gazelle to jackal; after three minutes she lost to jade, leopard to swan: in her mind, now, the web was fantastic, woven of light and dark, wide and high as a temple, and denser by the move.

She moved an elephant; jade lost again to ruby, gazelle to vulture; she, to ruby, leopard to jackal; she drew on the hookah and pondered, reaching out to adjust the positions of the pieces minutely before deciding, and picking up and placing her daughter.

And lost her, almost at once, to ruby, who sacrificed a vulture to the creation of a gambit Saphique bit her lip not to have seen.

After that, she was cautious, reserving her forces, half-allying with ruby for the destruction of jade, who went quickly and had been eaten away to queen, swan, two dolphins, two gazelles when Saphique put out her strength against ruby.

At first, success: the sacrifice of a swan to break a screen of jackals around the ruby daughter, and a jade dolphin had taken the daughter two moves later, then fallen to a python that Saphique had taken for the loss of a leopard; then a ruby high priestess to an eagle, and the ruby queen, who had marauded amongst the ranks of Saphique's leopards in mid-

board, was forced back to a corner to which Saphique laid siege in alliance with jade.

Then the beginning of the end: jade, feinting treachery to twist open a gateway in the ranks of Saphique's assault, through which a dolphin went forward for a vulture; and the dolphin, two moves later, took an eagle, and ruby broke the siege with counterflanking python and vulture, taking a leopard and gazelle, and forcing on the marble queen in her turn a retreat, and the withdrawal of eagle and elephants for a screen.

Almost on the hour the last-but-one of the jade pieces fell: a dolphin, leaving only the queen, who could not herself be taken with two sides remaining, only captured to one side or other: and the capture went to ruby, who sacrificed python and twin jackals for the prize.

And this was the end for Saphique, though she fought very hard for a true stalemate, or even that variant of a stalemate known as enslavement, in which a queen sacrifices all her remaining pieces in the space of no more or less than three moves, and so avoids immediate capture, but cannot make a further move without being captured.

Finally, on the LCD screen, Queen's python four to daughter's vulture eight; and Saphique slapped over the hookah, snatched up her queen and overturned the game in three violent, precise gestures.

She knelt, holding the piece in her lap, head bowed.

# Twenty-Four

They had taken a knife apiece on the corner of the *Vía*, holding the piece of cardboard and plastic between them, shielding it from sight. Now, standing at the bottom of the stairs, they were suddenly aware of the knives, tucked inside their belts.

Leaving the bag of shopping where it was, they climbed the first flight of stairs. On the landing there was a row of metal mail-boxes. FLAT 3, in the same neat black pen.

They climbed the next flight. Somewhere above, a door slammed. They waited to hear if footsteps would start descending the stairs. There was a clicking noise from the lights on the stairs.

Beside that, nothing.

They climbed the next flight.

Reached the next landing.

A frosted glass window along one wall, letting in light from the street.

Next to it, a white door.

Flat 3.

The lights clicked.

And went out.

Alanna said, "Now."

Sansiega started to pick the lock.

Sharp little clicks and pops of metal as she worked at the lock.

Her breath, softly getting faster, harder.

The sound of distant traffic.

Alanna's bladder swelled and tightened, drum-like, inside her belly.

The lock cracked, finally, and the door swung and stopped, caught on a chain inside. No light spilled out onto the corridor.

Alanna murmured and nudged Sansiega away from the door.

She drew the knife and put her head to the dark line of the opening, listening.

Her nose tickled with mustiness, the smell of old cooking, a smell of faint decay.

She reached through and fumbled at the chain.

This is what he's waited for. He'll slam the door on your hand now.

Smash it.

The chain came off the hook and swung, clicking, against the door-jamb.

She pushed at the door gently with her foot and it yawned darkness on her.

She listened, staring forward into the darkness, and heard only breathing. From behind her.

Sansiega.

She stepped inside, knife held forward, pointing upwards, her free hand roving the wall beside the door.

The light switch clicked under her finger and the flat was full of light. She relaxed a little.

In front of her was a big room, rectangular. In the opposite wall there was another door, open. Beyond it she could see cupboards and half of a gas-cooker.

She walked into the room.

To the left of the kitchen door there were shelves covered in books; there was a tall bookcase beside the TV and video at one end of the room. The lowest shelf was packed with video tapes. In front of the TV there was an armchair, zebra-striped in yellow and green and pulled to one side as though someone had got out of it it quickly. There was another chair to the left of the kitchen door, a wooden one with metal legs. A pot-plant sat on it, green-white, sprawling spiderishly.

The carpet was red, scuffed and dirty-looking; in the middle of the room there was a table, bare, scratched wood; underneath the table there was a big square box; at the opposite end of the room to the TV and video there was an altar, wide and high as the wall, in three sections.

On left and right, on waist-high shelves, there were figures, icons, statuettes of Artemis and Sita and Athena and Blodeuwedd and Isis and Lakshmi and Freyja; in the centre, on a head-high shelf, there were figures, icons, statuettes of Cybele and Durga and Ishtar and Hel and Kali.

Directly beneath this highest shelf, on a wide base covered with white cloth, there was a metre-high statue of a composite Goddess, a third human, a third fish, a third insect, limbs and fins and antennae lifted and turned in a frozen dance of threat and reassurance, dismissal and beckoning, blessing and curse. It was painted, the cool ganotic blues and greens and golds of the fish and insect thirds blended skilfully into the creamy whites and yellows and reds of the human.

Very easily, the head of the Goddess might have been repulsive or risible, a cramming of oval human eye with round fish with crystalline insect, of lips and nose with proboscis and snout, of skin and hair with bristles and scales; but it was neither: it was inhuman, *ahuman*, but beautiful.

Brass bowls crowded with the skeletal white ash of incense sticks were arranged on the white cloth before and between the feet and mandibles and fins, and there was a small white mat embroidered with moons in various phases in golden thread on the floor before it.

"She is beautiful."

Alanna jumped a little.

She turned.

Sansiega was staring at the statue, knife hanging loosely in her left hand.

In her wide eyes, the pupils were big, drugged-looking.

Alanna said, "Wake up!"

It was only half a joke.

Alanna walked across the room to the door of the kitchen.

She switched on the light.

It was empty, clean, but the faint smell of decay was stronger here.

Something black ran along the skirting board and vanished.

A cockroach.

The fridge hummed complacently in front of her.

She stared at it, suddenly fascinated.

Thinking.

Her stomach rolled inside her.

She turned back to the main room.

Where was the bathroom?

Probably a shared one, on the next landing.

She looked at the books on the shelves next to the kitchen door.

Novels.

Medical books, in Spanish and Basque; some of them, fewest, in English.

Books on war.

She noticed suddenly that they were arranged alphabetically by title, starting at 'Q'.

'Q' for *"Quemaduras, El Tratamiento de"*.

'P' for "Pathology, Basic".

She walked over to the books by the TV.

Novels.

Medical books.

Books on war.

Arranged alphabetically by author, starting at 'A'.

'A' for *"Abnormalidades Neurológicos"*.

'B' for *"Buchenwald, Experimentación Medical en"*.

She looked at the video tapes.

They were labelled in black felt pen.
Arranged alphabetically.
A B C.
*Atenas.*
*Berlín.*
*Cherburgo.*
D F G.
*Dunkerque.*
*Florencia.*
*Génova.*
Sansiega came up behind her.
There was a gap in the line of video-tapes.
T.
There was a tape cover on the seat of the armchair.
She picked it up.
'T' for *"Tolón".*
She switched the TV on and picked up the remote control from on top of the video. She pushed a button. The video whirred and a video tape slid half-out. She pushed it back in, and pressed PLAY.
The screen was white with static for a moment, then shook and unfolded with the image of a man's head and shoulders. The face was upturned, the mouth a foreshortened oval, chanting.
Then the chanting stopped and blood began to pour onto the head from above in a thick stream. Music was playing in the background, a heavy thumping drone with occasional irregular shouting in some language she didn't recognise.
The blood started to lessen in volume, coming in long thin spurts. The man shook his head from side to side and his wet hair swung and flew, aspergilling the air with red. He stepped forward, out of shot, and after a moment the image swung, revealing that the film was being taken in what looked like a disused warehouse or burnt-out building. The image bounced and settled into a new position and a man's body came into shot at the top of the screen as though being lowered from midair.
It was upside down, the arms strapped to the torso and the head covered in a white plastic bag with the letters S, P, R, M, A, C, and H visible on it. The bag was tied around tightly around the neck with twine and bulged and shook as though it was full of liquid. A plastic tube had been pushed into it beneath the twine, and blood was still streaming thinly from the end of the tube.
More of the body was lowered into shot.

114

It was naked.

The flaccid genitals liberated against the urine-sheened belly.

The body stopped lowering and the man who had chanted came back into shot. He was wearing a huge leather mask on his head. He lifted a knife, reaching for the gently swinging body.

Alanna switched the video off.

She knew what happened next.

Sansiega started to walk up the room towards the statue.

Alanna's eyes followed her.

The box under the table.

Alanna walked towards the table and bent down to pull the box out.

It wasn't as heavy as it looked.

She lifted it and put it on top of the table.

Lifted the lid off.

Inside the box there was thin white paper, wrapped around something.

She smelt leather, chemicals.

Faintly, decay.

She pulled at the paper, revealing what was below.

A head.

A leather head.

A gilded leather head.

She pulled it out and put it on the table beside the box, pulling the last pieces of paper away.

Not a head. A mask.

The blank eyeholes stared at her.

A pig mask.

*Sus scrofa.*

A boar's mask.

It seemed to have been made of many small pieces of leather, sewn together with precise little rows of stitches.

Coarse, grainy leather, dotted with little papillae.

Gilded.

The tusks jutted forward on either side.

She thought they were made of bone.

Ulnae.

She realized where the leather was from, and a woman's voice began speaking Spanish behind her. Not Sansiega's. A rich, contralto voice in which there seemed to buzz and hum and whisper the sound of wings and water and the wind amongst leaves.

Sansiega was kneeling in front of the Goddess statue on the white mat, hands laid palm-down on her breasts. The voice was coming out of the statue.

When it had finished, Sansiega stood up and turned around.

She said, "It was giving instructions. To him. The King. Telling him to go to England. What to do."

Alanna walked forward and knelt down on the white mat.

There was a faint whirring from the statue and the voice began to speak again.

*"Escucha bien, mi hijo..."*

She stood up and walked forward to the statue.

The voice continued.

She took hold of the statue. It seemed to be made of papier-mâché, but was heavy, weighted perhaps at its base. It rocked a little as she tried to move it.

She looked around.

"Help me," she said.

Together, they lifted the statue from the base.

The voice was coming from the base directly beneath where the statue had rested.

Alanna drew the white cloth away.

The base was made of wood, but there was a rectanglar hole in the middle, covered with a sheet of glass and filled with wires and electronic gadgets. There was a cassette in one corner resting in what looked like a dismantled tape recorder. Its spools were turning. The voice finished speaking and parts of the dismantled tape recorder flicked up and down like teeth. The cassette rewound, jerked a little and lay still.

The glass cover was hinged, and there was a small hole drilled in the opposite edge. Alanna put her finger into it and lifted the cover up. It rested on its hinges. She reached down into the rectangular hole and tried to lift the cassette out.

She became aware that something was trickling from her ears. Her eyes were closed. She opened them. She was lying down. Sansiega's foot lay in front of her face. Her head ached and her right hand felt as though it was broken.

She sat up and touched a finger of her left hand into the liquid trickling from her left ear. It was blood.

She looked at the base. Smoke was rising from it. The glass cover, still resting on its hinges, was streaked with yellow and white.

She looked at Sansiega. She was lying as though asleep, bald head tilted. A thin line of blood was shining on the skin beneath one of her ears.

The other ear was hidden against the floor.

Slowly, Alanna stood up. The contents of the rectangular hole were still mostly intact, but everything was streaked with the yellow and white stains, which radiated out from the buckled remnants of the tape as though something had exploded beneath it.

Something had.

So why weren't they dead?

She looked at her right hand.

Tried gingerly, to move it.

It felt as though it had been caught in a door after all.

But she could move it, just about.

She squatted beside Sansiega.

With her free hand, she gently tugged at her shoulder.

She started to speak.

"Are you.."

And realized for the first time that she couldn't hear anything.

# Twenty-Five

The house was at the end of the road, shielded by trees from its nearest neighbour. He parked on the driveway and took out his luggage. Later, he'd find out which of the keys fitted the door to the garage.

It wasn't the big Yale. That was for the house.

He pushed the door open and walked inside. The house was filled with cool silence. There was a small table just inside the door; above it, a mirror; next to it, a white coat-tree and an umbrella rack with a single black umbrella in it.

He carried his suitcase through the first door and put it against the wall.

*La sala de estar.*

TV, video, bookcases.

Later, he'd see what She had provided for him.

For now, he needed to see Her in person.

Where was She?

He glanced into the kitchen.

Electric cooker, lino floor, sink, washing machine.

Which reminded him.

He stripped off his trousers, wrapped them into a ball and tossed them at the washing machine. They slid to a halt almost in front of it.

Crumbs of mud lay scattered on the floor behind them.

He'd mop the floor before he left.

He went upstairs in his underpants, bare legs swinging easily three steps at a time. Opened the first door on the left.

And had found Her.

He knelt on the threshold, head bowed, and prayed silently.

The strip of metal dividing the red carpet in the corridor from the white inside the room cut into his knees.

He savoured the pain, drawing it up into his head to season the silent syllables of the prayer.

When the prayer was over he climbed to his feet and walked slowly into the room.

Now, She would speak to him.

He knelt on the white mat that lay on the floor before Her, embroidered with moons in golden thread.

A faint, mosquito humming.

*"Escucha bien, mi hijo..."*

# Twenty-Six

A tear of fresh blood had crept down the lobe of Sansiega's ear, coloured strangely under the overhead light. She lay with her body turned towards the window, head resting against a pillow propped on the wall.
The tear wasn't moving.
It must have been the change in pressure when the plane took off.
Alanna looked away, back at the pad whose pages she had been turning. Alternate lines in green and red biro.
Their conversations, hers and Sansiega's, since they had left the Ripper's flat. She looked at the last page they had written on, the pad propped on the armrest between them.

— What city was it?
— I don't remember. A city in the north. The north-east, I think.
— Leeds? Hull? York? Sheffield? Huddersfield?
— I don't remember. *Verdaderamente.*
— What does that mean?
— I don't remember. It's another one. It's the opposite of wrong. An *adverbio.*
— Does it mean 'truly'?
— Yes. Truly. Truly, I don't remember.
— OK. Don't worry. Sleep if you want to.

So she had slept, and Alanna had turned the pages of the pad and then looked at her and seen the tear of blood. Sansiega was ill. It was obvious. When the explosion in the flat had blown them unconscious (Alanna thought now that only the detonator had gone off, not the main charge), she must have banged her head, hard, on the floor.
She too was deaf, but also she complained of feeling sleepy, of sometimes seeing coloured halos around objects and people. And she was forgetting her English: words were seeping away into her subconcious, as though her English were grains of coloured sand sprinkled on the hard glossy pebbles of her Spanish. Some fell into the dark interstices of unremembering between the pebbles; others, incongruously, sat safe in the light atop a pebble. She could remember the word "fingernail" but she'd forgotten all colour terms; she knew the

120

numbers but had forgotten how to form ordinals.

Alanna turned the pages back and read the conversation they'd had when they got back to the car, taking the pad and pens from the bag they'd bought them in and writing quickly, handing the pad back and forward.

— You need to go to a hospital.
— NO. We have to catch him.
— You're hurt.
— I'm not bad. I have a little *sueño*. I don't remember the word English.
— I can hunt him by myself. YOU NEED TO GO TO A HOSPITAL.
— No. I don't remember the *instructiones*, all of them. But I will maybe remember more. If I am not with you, you will miss him. It is the same. It is the same *todavía*. You need me.

Alanna remembered sitting without moving for long time, the pad resting on her knees, then writing quickly, angrily.

— OK. I'll drive. We'll catch the next plane back. If you start feeling worse, tell me.

Sansiega had read, smiled at her. Mouthed, "OK, good. *Vamos*." Let's go.

And here they were, on their way back. They had bought the tickets in a travel agency Sansiega knew in Bilbao. Expensive, but quick. Sansiega had done the talking. Later, she had said (written) that it had been strange to speak and hear nothing, just feel your voice buzzing in your throat.

The travel agent had been very helpful, but Alanna wondered how long before the police would be questioning her. They had got out of the flat and into the street only thirty seconds or so before police cars came sliding down the middle of the street, lights flashing.

From the way other people's heads were turning, the sirens must have been wailing like banshees, but they heard nothing. Then one of the police cars stopped and an officer with a machine-gun slung over his shoulder jumped out and put a megaphone to his lips.

Then everyone started running. They ran too. Little knots of people had gathered outside buildings, presumably when the explosion sounded. It couldn't have been very loud, but loud enough. People were running away from the King's flat. The policeman must have said that it was a terrorist bomb. ETA. By now they maybe knew the truth.

And *they* would know that she had done more than turn down their offer. Had they guessed she would? Had they set up the booby-trap in the flat to kill her?

No. No, how could they have known that Sansiega would show her how to get the King's address?

But no, they could. The fax machine must have been bugged.

So had they been watched since they went to Spain?

To make certain nothing went wrong?

It was possible.

Maybe that was why the police were so quick to respond to reports of the explosion.

Maybe.

Maybe.

Everything was maybe.

Would the police be able to reconstruct the tape?

She didn't think so. Maybe when they tried to examine the thing in the first place, the booby-trap would go off properly.

Maybe.

Her head ached.

Beside her, Sansiega moved in her sleep. Her lips worked.

She was saying something aloud.

Maybe something about the instructions.

Saying something aloud.

Silently.

Alanna folded back the top page of the pad for a fresh one.

She started to write.

# Twenty-Seven

He stood in the shadow of the trees and watched the house.

She had told him of three possible targets.

This was the first of them.

He had been waiting ten minutes. After another twenty, he would try the second.

The trees were at the back of the house. Maybe the target was there, in a room at the front, all this time, and he couldn't see it. But it was too risky to watch the front.

Better to stand here and wait, watching to see if one of the dark windows lightened.

And one did. A small one, on the second floor.

He climbed over the low fence and ran through the garden, past the greenhouse, the flowerbeds, to the house.

He flattened himself against it, arms high, and stared up at the light directly above. He heard the sound of a lavatory flushing, faintly. A moment later the light flicked off.

He dragged a rubbish bin along to the kitchen and stood on it to break the smaller top pane in one of the windows. The glass fell inwards loudly. He knocked out the remaining shards and leaned inside a long arm through to undo the catch at the bottom.

Stupid old bitch.

It was so easy.

Just as She had told him it would be.

He climbed through the window and jumped to the floor.

Shards of glass were lying on the floor.

One of them was perfect.

Shaped like a spearhead, almost.

Like the spearhead that had pierced the side of the Usurper.

He wrapped his hand in a cloth that was hanging on a hook on the wall (*Butterflies of the British Isles*) and picked up the shard. It fitted snugly.

He swung it in front of him.

Perfect.

He opened the kitchen door.

A short corridor.

Stairs.

A door, ajar.

Flickering light spilled through it.

The sound of an aircraft, very loud.

Two strides took him to the door and through it.

Thinking about it afterwards, he wondered if she even had time to realize that she was being killed.

Inside the room, left to right, from the door.

A wall with two pictures on it.

A big television.

A tub of flowers.

Curtains, tightly drawn.

Bookshelves.

Photos along the mantelpiece above an electric fire.

A sofa.

An armchair.

A fat, stupid old bitch.

Red, flowery dress.

Round glasses.

A hearing aid.

Mouth gaping wetly in surprise.

His arm rammed across her throat.

He felt cartilages breaking under it.

Cricoid.

Thyroid.

The hyoid bone.

His other hand came up and round in an arc.

Light flashed on the shard of glass.

It went home into the fat swelling of the belly just above the mons pubis.

Despite his strangle-hold, air whooshed from the gaping, silenced mouth.

Flecks of saliva splattered his face.

Her breath smelt stale, like wet old bones.

He thrust the shard in further, shifting his feet for more power.

And began to saw upwards.

Blood sprayed out around his hand.

It felt as though he had thrust it into a loose, boiling vagina.

The tip of the shard had reached the fundus of the uterus, puncturing the recently emptied bladder.

It travelled upwards, up into the sigmoid colon.

In the face, the mouth filled suddenly with blood.

It ran over the lips in thin separate streams.

His hand squelched and farted liquidly, moving upwards through the gut.

Colon sigmoid.

Colon transverse.

Caecum.

Ileum.

Jejunum.

Pylorus.

Stomach.

The blood vessels.

The superior and inferior mesenteric.

The superior haemorrhoides.

Inferior pancreatico-duodenal.

Ileo-colic.

The vasa intestini tenuis.

Colicae dextra.

Media.

Sinistra.

The sigmoides.

His arm was wet as far as the shoulder with blood.

The hot tang of it was mixed with the stink of faeces.

Thick glistening fluids poured from the slashed open vessels of the guts.

He pulled his hand free with a long pop.

*Sostenuto.*

She poured through the great slash he had opened for her.

*Andantino.*

He took his arm away from her throat.

Her head fell sideways.

*Adante.*

Blood splashed inside the mouth.

Her dentures had come loose, protruding a centimetre or so beyond the lips.

Red saliva dripped from the lowest edge.

He stood back, smiling, eyes wide.

Blood was running down his face like sweat.

His tongue crept out, licking at it.

Blessed be.

O, blessed be!

# Twenty-Eight

From Heathrow they caught the shuttle to Newcastle. Sansiega was worse. She had started to suffer headaches, brief spasms of intense, viced-in pain. Her hands were trembling all the time, fine, almost imperceptible tremors interspersed during the headaches an irregular carphology, a random twisting and clutching of her own clothes, Alanna's, the arm of her chair.

It was becoming difficult to read what she wrote. Alanna had bought a bottle of painkillers at the duty-free supermarket, and on the flight Sansiega had taken three of them.

— *Estoy* little better. A little.
— Have you remembered any more?
— No. *Nada.*

As she guided Sansiega towards the taxi ranks, Alanna stopped to buy a paper. She handed over the money and the woman at the kiosk looked at it and said something to her. She shook her head, indicating her ear. The woman held the coin up, twisting it between forefinger and thumb to show both sides of it. She'd handed over a 100-*peseta* coin by mistake.

Her English change was in her other pocket. She took the coin back and tried to reach the pocket. Sansiega was holding onto her arm. She disengaged her gently and pulled out a handful of change.

She selected a fifty-pence piece.

"I'm sorry. I'm very tired."

The woman shrugged, looking away.

She folded the newspaper in half and pushed it into her shoulder bag and turned away from the kiosk. Sansiega stood waiting for her. She walked to her and took her hand, nodding forward at the taxis and smiling.

The head of the taxi-driver swung on the other side of the glass, presenting her with his profile.

Had he spoken?

She said, "City centre."

The head swung back and the taxi started up.

She sat back in the seat, releasing a long breath.

126

She felt tired and dirty.
Her eyes were sore and she could hardly move her injured hand.
But there was still everything to do, and she didn't even know if they had started yet.
No rest for the wicked.
No rest for the hunters of the wicked.
Ha, ha.
Sansiega was looking out of the window.
Alanna pulled the pad out and wrote on it.

— Do you want another painkiller?

She showed the pad to Sansiega, who shook her head.
The taxi stopped at an intersection. It was raining and reflections of car headlamps, the traffic lights, street lamps, lay everywhere on slick wet surfaces like puddles of body fluid, blood, piss, faeces.
The lights changed and the taxi slid forward.
She watched the streets go by. At the far end of one street she caught a glimpse of a woman in a raincoat running, frozen against the pale evening sky. The bright windows of a Chinese takeaway went by, crowded with black expectant outlines. She looked at her watch and started practicing again, moving her lips silently as she said the words. Would she even be able to understand her? *Christina*, it was fifteen years. Kids' games.
Another intersection. The driver's head swung sideways in front of her. His lips moved.
What the fuck had he said?
"I don't know," she said.
The head swung back.
It was OK.
The lights changed and the taxi slid forward.
Two minutes later she leaned forward to the grill in the glass panel.
"Here," she said.
The taxi pulled over.
She tugged at Sansiega's arm and the bald head came away from the window, eyes narrow.
She paid the fare and watched the taxi drive away.
The rain was coming in cold, icy flurries. Her breath steamed.
She took Sansiega's hand and walked her to the bus shelter, sat her down on the driest seat. When she was in the telephone booth she

twisted around so she could watch the shelter. Sansiega's head was bowed, as though she were sleeping again.

She fed a pound coin into the slot and punched the number.

The earpiece of the phone felt cold against her ear.

She waited two seconds and started speaking.

"Susan? Listen, it's me, Alanna. Susan? Listen, it's me, Alanna. Don't talk. I can't hear you."

She repeated the words, staring at the dark shape inside the bus-shelter.

After about thirty seconds she took a breath and started talking again.

"Susan, I need your help. I want you to go to Tig's house at once. Remember Tig? Borrow her car. Come to pick me up. I'm waiting near the pub where Joanna was sick that time. Remember, just after Mel's divorce? And for the Goddess's sake, bring something to eat. Something for two people. I don't think they can be watching all the entrances to your block. Be careful. And please, hurry."

She repeated the instructions until her money ran out.

She left the booth.

Another ten minutes and I'll try again.

Sansiega was sleeping, head hanging slackly on her neck. White puffs of breath bloomed irregularly on her lips. She was talking again.

Alanna skimmed water off the seat next to her and sat down, shivering. She pulled the paper from the bag and spread it on her knees. Her stomach lurched.

On the front page, next to a photograph of an old woman that looked as though it had been cut from a larger one, the headline said, *HAS IT STARTED HERE?*

She read the story, shivering.

When she had finished, she folded the paper and put it back into the bag. She hugged herself, watching the traffic, thinking about what she would do if Susan didn't come.

After ten minutes she got up and went back into the booth.

As she started the instructions for the second time, she saw an orange Ford station wagon pull out of a line of traffic at the far end of the road and come driving slowly along the pavement.

She leaned out of the booth, waving, still speaking into the mouthpiece. The Ford stopped beside the bus-shelter.

Alanna slammed the phone into its cradle and spilled herself out of the booth. The driver had got out of the car and come running around to the front. A plump, short-haired woman in jeans and jersey.

Alanna was shaking Sansiega gently awake. She looked up as the woman

128

came through the entrance to the shelter.

"Fucking hell, Susan, I have never been so glad to see anyone in my life."

She was crying a little as she said it.

Susan's lips moved.

Alanna helped Sansiega to her feet.

"No, don't say anything. I can't hear anything. Need a bit more practice in lip-reading. Can you take her?"

She picked up Sansiega's bag.

Susan guided Sansiega to the car, opened one of the back doors and helped her inside. She left the door open for Alanna and walked to the bonnet of the car, waited for a break in the traffic and ran round, opened the door and jumped inside.

Alanna closed the door.

The inside of the car smelt of incense and cigarette smoke; after a moment, of freshly cooked rice. Susan fastened her seat-belt and turned around in her seat, gesturing into the space at the back of the car. Alanna looked and saw a white plastic bag.

She leaned over and picked it up.

It was heavy and warm.

The car pulled away from the kerb.

Alanna was pulling the foil boxes of Chinese food from the bag. She felt into the bottom of the bag and pulled out two plastic forks. Sansiega was watching her. She put a fork into her hand and pulled the cardboard top off one of the boxes. Thin, slow steam poured up from the flat surface of the rice. Her mouth watered. She swallowed, putting the box on Sansiega's lap and reaching for a box for herself.

With her mouth full of rice she said, "This is so good I'll think I'm going to have an orgasm."

Sansiega was eating quickly, rice dropping from her fork.

When they stopped at a traffic light, Susan turned around and spoke, moving her lips exaggeratedly. She repeated herself.

"Where do you want to go?"

Alanna swallowed, wiping her lips carefully with her injured hand.

The lights changed and the car slid forward.

"I need a gun. The Slaughter King is in England. You know the killing in York? It was him. I have to stop him. When we stop, we can talk. You write, I'll talk. Do you know somewhere I can get a gun?"

Susan's head swung up and down.

They drove for half-an-hour, leaving Newcastle and heading north.

Sansiega was sleeping again. As the car turned off the road and bumped along a rough road leading up to what looked like a farmhouse, Alanna gathered up the remains of the takeaway meal, screwing the empty containers into balls and dropping them into the white plastic bag.

The car stopped outside the front door of the house. Susan got out. A light came on inside the porch and the door opened. A dog came running out, followed by a middle-aged woman in a shapeless white dress.

On the edge of the circle of light from the porch, she and Susan hugged each other. They broke the embrace. Susan was talking quickly. The woman looked towards the car. Alanna popped the doorhandle and got out.

As she walked up, the woman stepped back into the light and started to speak in sign-language, smiling.

Alanna smiled back.

"You've caught me a couple of years too early. I'm Alanna."

They hugged.

The dog banged against Alanna's legs. She stooped to pat it, and turned back to the car to help Sansiega out.

A couple of minutes later she and Susan were sitting in a big kitchen, two cups of tea and a pad on the table in front of them. The woman, Marj, was upstairs, helping Sansiega to have a shower.

Susan wrote and pushed the pad in front of Alanna.

— How bad is she?

Alanna said, "She's bad. She injured her head in Spain. She needs to see a doctor, but she won't. She says I need her. She's right. If she remembers something else, it could be what I need to stop him."

— How are you going to do it?

"Sansiega says the instructions told him to stay in York two days and then go west. She's trying to remember the route. I think today is his second day. If she remembers in time, we're going to wait on the road for him to go by."

— What!? How are you going to know what car is his?

"Faith. That's all we've got left. Without that, we might as well give up."

130

— Why can't you go to the police?

"It's too complicated to tell you. You can read it. I wrote everything down on the flight. I want you to take it to a friend of mine in Edinburgh. A journalist. They'll expect you to go to London."
Susan waved her hand and wrote quickly.

— Who's "they"?

"You'll know when you read it. You'll understand then. Have you said anything to Marj about a gun?"

— Yes. She can let you have a shotgun. With lots of ammo.

"OK. Good. *Christina*, I need to sleep."

# Twenty-Nine

He had three hours left. Would She give him more lives?

Earlier in the day he had gone into the city centre and bought a tourist guide. He didn't think She would have wanted him to do it — why else would She have provided him with the videos, the books? — but killing the old woman the night before hadn't satisfied him.

He had wanted to spend more time with the corpse, arranging it to his satisfaction, perhaps exploring the sexual possibilities of the great overflowing vertical mouth he had opened in the guts.

But he could not. She had told him not to.

After the killing, he had showered quickly upstairs and left, pausing only long enough to take his souvenir from the corpse. But even that, later, in the bathroom of the house She had provided for him, hadn't been able to drain the excitement that had dammed up inside him. Afterwards, he had been unable to sleep.

Thus, the tourist guide.

Thus, the hours spent memorizing street names and routes.

Thus, the car parked on a curve of Micklegate at ten fifteen, and he stepping from it.

A minute before, as he parked, a group of youths, drunk and loud, had been walking past on the pavement. It was cold but they were wearing thin shirts, football shirts (Leeds United, Celtic, even Barcelona), and jeans. They had seen him and one of them had put his face hard to the passenger window, rolling his eyes and twisting his face.

When he had pulled away, his lips and tongue had left thick white stains against the window that slowly oozed downwards. Watching, he had begun to shake with anger and disgust, but he had only smiled. After the youths had gone, he sat in the car, letting the emotions build inside him, fuelling his will for the hoped-for slaughter.

But the possibility of it had been slow in materializing.

He had walked through the streets, twice seeing a possibility, twice beginning to stalk, twice frustrated. He ended up a long way from the city centre. Cars slid past. No pedestrians. He had a drink in a small pub, biting the beer down rather than swallowing it, and started to walk back to his car.

He walked straight through the city centre. Another group of youths shouted something at him from the other side of the road but when he'd turned and gestured to them, foolishly, they had only laughed.

And what if they hadn't?

He could have taken them.

They were cowards and they were drunk.

As soon as he had spilled one of them onto the pavement, they would have run.

But it would have been so stupid.

Killing in public.

He reached his car and got in, looking up the street one last time.

There were two night-clubs on the street, wide mouths ulcerated with vivid neon. Music thumped from within the bright throats. People were eaten and regurgitated, standing in small groups on the wet pavement, crouched and stamping against the cold.

Wind trembled against the car and he heard the distant clanging of an ambulance. A couple emerged from the nearest nightclub, the one on his side of the street, and came walking slowly towards him, leaning against each other. As they got closer he saw that they were both women, one thinner, taller, the other fatter, shorter. The thinner one was wearing a *Clitoridectoma* T-shirt underneath her coat. Both of them had short hair. They were talking and looked a little drunk.

He waited for them to go well past and got out of the car.

They were about twenty metres away, about to walk through the right-hand arch of the big stone gates at the end of Micklegate. He walked quickly, suddenly afraid he was going to lose them.

He passed through the arch and stood on the corner of Queen Street. They had carried straight on, down Blossom Street. He crossed to the other side of the road. A taxi went past with a starred back window. Ahead of him, they were standing at a zebra crossing, almost slumped against each other for support. He sat on the low brick wall of the car-park and watched them out of the corner of his eye. His stomach glowed yeastily with excitement.

They crossed the road. He waited, then got up and walked after them. They turned off down a sidestreet and he started to run.

Already they could be opening a door and stepping inside. He reached the mouth of the sidestreet. Sixth or seventh house down, on the opposite side, a shin-booted leg lifted from the pavement and was taken through the door. The soft sound of the door closing carried clearly to him. He crossed over and walked down the street, failure curdling coldly inside his warm stomach.

But how the fuck could you have expected anything else?

Doing this, you are disobeying Her.

How could you have expected anything else?

Ahead of him, light poured through a downstairs window in the house.

Just before he drew level with the window, a curtain came across it. He heard it rattle, and spat.

He could ring the bell.

*Hombre*, they were drunk, but not that drunk.

So, they let you come in and have your wicked way with them, and say nothing, shout nothing?

Do you want a miracle?

Disobeying Her, you want *un milagro?*

He passed the house.

He thought suddenly, what if there is *una callejuela*, an alley, down the back?

There was.

It was narrow.

Dark.

Smelt of dog piss.

He walked along it, counting houses.

Stood behind the sixth house from the far end, staring at the back wall over a wooden fence.

A window was open on the second floor, and there was a drain-pipe.

He climbed the fence and walked across the rain-wet cement of the back-yard.

He kept low, moving quickly.

He squatted against the wall.

Stood up.

The ground floor window looked into the kitchen.

It was dark inside the house.

He took off his shoes and socks and put them in a corner of the yard.

The cement was freezing beneath the bare soles of his feet.

He went to stand beneath the drain-pipe.

Flexed his toes and fingers.

Wiped the sole of each foot dry against the trouser of the opposite leg.

And started to climb.

About two-thirds of the way up, the pipe branched, the main part of it carrying straight up, a smaller bending to the left at forty-five degrees, to the window he had noticed ajar.

When he reached the fork he rested a moment, clinging to the pipe with hands and feet. He looked behind him. On the other side of the alley an almost identical row of back walls faced him. Lights were on here and then, pearly through curtains.

He grabbed hold of the angled pipe and slowly, lifting his feet one by one away from the main pipe, released his weight onto it.

Metal creaked.

It held.

Face to the wall, he swung along the pipe, putting his feet together and penduluming them gently to help himself along. When he was nearly at the window he grabbed hold of the sill with his left hand, and lifting his body up and sideways until he could grip the pipe between his knees.

He inched nearer the window, then, holding the pipe tightly with his right hand, he reached inside through the gap to lift the catch. It was stiff and he could only use his fingers to work at it.

His whole body trembled with strain.

When the catch came up with a little snick, the window swung outwards and he nearly lost balance.

His forehead went cold with sweat.

He nudged the window fully open and put his left arm through it, reaching for the edge of the inside sill.

For a second, he trusted his whole weight to the sill. He felt the frame of the window shake, and then he had his other arm and his upper body through. His legs dangled behind him in the open air.

It was the window of the bathroom.

His eyes adjusted to the shadows.

Directly below him was a lavatory with a fluffy cover. There was a sink, a medicine cabinet and mirror, and, on the back of the door, a poster of Margaret Thatcher in the pose popularized by Che Guevara.

He kicked and pulled himself further inside.

The window was too small for him to get his legs up and round in front of him. He lowered his upper body inside until he was able to rest his hands on the lavatory seat for a few seconds and get his breath. Then he slid forward into the room as quietly as he could, slowing himself by snagging his knees and feet on the window frame.

Inelegant, but effective.

He got to his feet and closed the window, then walked to the door and laid his ear to Margaret Thatcher's cheek, listening.

He opened the door a centimetre at a time, looked out, opened it fully, and walked out onto a carpeted corridor, at the end of which he could see the top of a flight of stairs.

Darkness.

Silence.

There were two doors along the corridor, both of them open.

He put his head slowly around the first.

A bedroom. Empty. Double bed. Make-up table. *Leucorrhoea* poster on one wall. Clothes were laid untidily on the bed.

He walked to the second door.

An office. Bookshelves. Computer. Calendar.

He went to the top of the stairs and listened down into the darkness below.

Nothing.

He climbed the stairs one at a time, holding firmly onto the stair-rail.

There was a coat over the post at the end of the rail.

It was the one he had seen the thinner woman wearing.

It smelt of cigarette smoke.

One of the sleeves was damp.

He sniffed his fingers.

With beer.

He stood at the foot of the stairs.

To his left, there was a corridor running along the bottom of the stairs.

To his right, there was another open door.

Directly in front of him was the front door of the house.

It was bolted.

He looked through the door on the right.

It was the room he had seen the light come on in.

The curtains were drawn, the light off.

TV, sofa, bookshelves, two armchairs, a table with a telephone on it.

He turned to the left.

At the end of the corridor there was another door, half-open.

He pushed through it into the kitchen.

He could hear something now.

Faint bass rhythms coming through the floor.

He half heard them, half felt them in his feet.

On his left, in the kitchen wall, was a big wooden door.

It was shut.

Outlined with light.

When he put his hand to it, he could feel the bass in the palm.

He put his ear to the door.

He recognized the music.

*Gynaekophagia.*

"Long Sow".

They were down in the cellar.

He tested the door.

It was locked from the opposite side.

*Mierda.*

He stood, thinking.

He walked over to the cupboards and drawers, opening them and pulling them out. He put a plastic jug beside the sink, then various bowls, metal and ceramic.

He started to fill the jug from the cold water tap, almost to the top.

When it was ready, he carried it over to the door, putting it one side of the door, near the hinges.

One by one he filled the other containers and carried them to the door. When he was finished, he picked up the jug, squatted beside the door, and started to pour the water underneath it, slowly but steadily. Then a metal bowl. Another metal bowl.

He laid the empty containers with the ones that were still full.

As he poured the fourth bowl of water, he heard the music turned down. Voices.

He put the bowl down.

Waited.

Footsteps splashing up a stair.

A lock, rattling.

By then, he was standing to one side of the door, feet placed among the bowls.

The door swung outwards, half-covering him.

The thinner woman walked into the kitchen.

She was wearing a PVC miniskirt and a leather jacket. Her hands and forearms glistened as though they were wet.

Surgical gloves.

She smelt of sweat.

He stepped out from behind the door.

His left foot hit one of the bowls with a half-musical clang.

She started to turn, but she was already dead.

*Tchlunk.*

He held her as she fell to the floor.

Underneath the leather jacket, she was naked.

Her nipples were pierced.

From each a little silver star of David hung.

They swung, glittering, as he lowered her.

The handle of the knife was black between them, like a nose between eyes.

He stood up from her and turned to the door of the cellar.

Light poured through it.

He took another knife from the cutlery drawer and walked down the steps, keeping his feet wide on the wet stone.

At the bottom of the steps his heart thudded.

Such a gift!

In the ceiling of the cellar burned a fluorescent tube.

Three walls, and the floor, were bare.

In one corner there was a stereo and racks of tapes.

Water glistened on the floor, slowly spreading out from the foot of the steps.

The fatter woman stood strapped against the fourth wall. She was naked, hooded. Her large nipples were swollen and vertical lips, dark pink, glistened beneath her shaved mon pubis.

Her skin was marked with bruises.

Rough with sweat.

There was a table to one side of her with a compartmented tray on top of it. Bottles of lubricant. Rings. Chains. Candles. A box with a red cross on the lid.

"What the fuck was it?"

The voice came muffled beneath the hood.

He walked over to the stereo and examined the tape-racks.

*Leucorrhoea.*

*Shrew.*

*Fishwife.*

*Clitoridectoma.*

"What was it?"

*Infibulatrix.*

*Dysmenorrhoea.*

*Mastectomy.*

He put the knife on top of the stereo, pressed STOP/EJ and replaced the *Gynaekophagia* with *Mastectomy*'s "Cheyne's Line".

F.FWD.

PLAY.

F.FWD.

PLAY.

REW.

"Jo, will you fucking well tell me what it was?"

PLAY.

138

He turned up the volume.

The distorted chain-saw samples of the fade-out to the second track filled the cellar.

She was shouting now.

He could just about hear her.

When the next track started, he wouldn't.

He climbed the steps and closed and locked the door.

Climbed down.

A second of silence, and then the triple-bass attack of "Mastect-o-Masochism-o" was howling inside the cellar. As he walked over to the stereo to pick up the knife he could see that it was vibrating, almost jumping into the air.

He picked it up and walked over to the woman.

She was struggling inside the bonds, scarcely moving.

He drew the musk of her terror through his nostrils, eyes closed.

He opened his eyes.

He took her left breast in his left hand and cut horizontally at a tangent to its upper curve, at about the level of the third rib.

He quickly took his hand away.

The cut was a centimetre or so deep.

Blood poured from it and down the breast in a sheet.

The sheet was divided by the nipple. Beneath it, a triangle of white skin showed against the red.

He swapped the knife from right to left hand and took the right breast in his right hand.

Cut horizontally at a tangent to its upper curve, at about the level of the third rib.

He quickly took his hand away.

The cut was a centimetre or so deep.

Blood poured from it and down the breast in a sheet.

The sheet was divided by the nipple. Beneath it, a triangle of white skin showed against the red.

The two sheets of blood trembled to the *Mastectomy* bass.

It had covered her as far down as the ankles now, and had started to puddle on the floor.

He watched it.

The woman was screaming something.

Her head rocked from side to side beneath the hood.

He could faintly hear what she was screaming beneath the *Mastectomy*.

A single word, over and over.

"Pineapple".

He stepped closer to her.

Made hooks of his hands and put the tips of his fingers, left, right, into the cuts, left, right.

Worked them deeper.

*Sawed* them deeper with his fingernails.

Through the superficial fascia into the muscle of the pectoralis major.

He felt the long hard bars of the ribs beneath his fingers.

Pushed his thumbs firmly into the skin beneath the cuts.

Drew a deep breath.

And tore her breasts off.

# Thirty

Twenty kilometres west of Harrogate, Alanna waited.

Sansiega suckled her left breast.

Marj had given them a car, a gun, and her blessing.

The car was a Honda hatchback, fast and manoeuvrable.

It was parked in a lay-by on the A-59, facing the traffic from Harrogate.

The gun was an illegal short-barrelled shotgun.

It sat on the back seat of the car, loaded.

The blessing had been brief, functional, and beautiful.

Neither of them had heard it.

After Marj had brought Sansiega down from upstairs, Sansiega said that she remembered more of the instructions.

Enough to know the route the King would take west.

When he would take it.

But she refused to tell Alanna, unless she was taken with her.

By then it was plain that Sansiega was very ill. Her eyes were sunken in circles of bruised purple flesh; occasionally, they blazed up into feverish brilliance, shining like superheated gems; more often, they were dull, as though turned inwards on the dark webs that nimble-limbed spiders of neurological damage were weaving within her skull. She was muttering to herself almost continuously now, asleep and awake.

Susan had told Alanna what it was she said.

Nothing.

And everything.

A trilingual glossolalia, words of Basque, Spanish and English, chopped and churned together with fervid illogic: Basque ergative suffixes mismated with Spanish pronominals, Spanish diminuatives with English proper nouns, English irregular plurals with rural Basque zoonomata; English was given gender; Spanish stripped of it; Basque rendered analytic; English agglutinative; Spanish clogged with double consonants; English blown free of aspirates; Basque drenched in liquids. It was as though inside her head the three oceans of her languages rose and warred above the ramparts and dykes that had divided them, mingling their separate waters in cataclysmic tsunamis that swept aside the fragile, sky-piercing crystal cities of her logic and sanity.

She was ill.

Very ill.

But Alanna could not refuse her.

They had driven very hard to reach the place at which they waited for the King. Perhaps they were already too late. Cars fled past, huge-eyed and anonymous in the darkness, and Alanna wondered how she would ever know the King's when it came, if it had not already boomed thunderously silent past her, a metal-skinned worm boring westward through the cool flesh of night to a new rottenness of slaughter.

He would come, and she would not know it.

He *had* come, and she had not known it.

And yet, in the midst of this hopelessness her faith was strong, like a tree throwing branches and leaves wide beneath a centuries-dark sky, blind in belief of a soon-to-come sun.

Sansiega's lips and teeth worked around her nipple.

There was no sex in the suckling.

Just a desire for comfort, and a desire to give it.

Sansiega had clung to her, her hot throat buzzing with endless words, and Alanna, watching the road, had stroked her face and temples, sweat sliding beneath her fingertips. Sansiega's mouth had closed over a finger, tongue and lips working at her own taste, teeth nipping softly, and Alanna had gently reclaimed the finger and offered her breast to the mouth.

The car was filled with the little noises of the suckling.

Wet pops and pips of sealing and unsealing.

Occasionally, they were flooded in the sound of a passing car, like stars drowned in the blazing of a witch-fired moon.

Alanna heard nothing.

Sansiega, a little.

Very slowly, her hearing was returning.

Very slowly, in the east, the sky was lightening.

At midday, in York, a police pathologist of twenty years' experience would be kneeling beneath the earth on rough cement, releasing the contents of his stomach in revolted tribute to the handiwork of the King that hung in fragments on the wall before him.

And the husk that had been the King, and would be again, as the salt tide of his needs were drawn up again into him by the dark moon of his madness, came west.

After he had finished with the woman strapped to the wall, he had climbed into the kitchen and stripped and washed himself clean at the sink, throwing his bloodsoaked clothes aside. Then, naked, he had climbed back down into the cellar and browsed through the cassette racks by the stereo.

He hadn't been familiar with some of the groups.

He had carried a double handful of them up the steps, and lain them beside the back yard door. He had then gone upstairs. Some of the clothes fitted him well. He had tossed a coin from the bedside table to see whether he should wear a *Dysmenorrhoea* or *Infibulatrix* T-shirt.

*¿Cruz o cara?*

*Cruz.*

*Infibulatrix.*

He had walked downstairs.

Found a plastic bag for his tapes.

Gone out into the back yard.

Put on his shoes and socks.

Climbed the back wall and returned to Her and Her house.

Wholly satisfied.

Souvenirless.

Now, he came west, playing one of his new tapes.

*Nekro-Femme.*

"Comfort Camp".

He had cranked the speakers up well past distortion point.

He could take or leave the percussion and vocals, but some of the bass work was excellent.

The wheel vibrated under his fingers.

He didn't see the Honda hatchback.

Alanna saw him.

Just another car.

But a second after he had passed, Sansiega's head came up from Alanna's breast and swung to follow his disappearing rear-lights. Her whole body had stiffened.

Her mouth was closed and silent.

A second later, her head dropped slowly back to the breast, mouth open again and mumbling.

Alanna took her gently by the nape of the neck and guided her away, gesturing her to do up her seatbelt. She leaned forward to turn on the engine, fastening up her blouse stiffly with her right hand.

She swung the car onto the road, hands moving with brief, decisive violence, and stood smoothly on the accelerator.

Her heart-rate had gone from the low fifties to the high one-twenties.

The red rear eyes of the King's car widened on the road ahead of her.

She waited until about twenty metres separated them.
The shot-gun stopped sliding backwards on the seat behind her.

# Thirty-One

The world's best sniper's rifle was designed by a myopic Moscow Dinamo fan who endured two sub-zero nights in a dinghy on the Baltic Ocean to escape the Soviet Union in the late 'Sixties.

It has provided a small but significant part of the revenue of the Swedish armaments industry for over twenty years.

Although it has been wedded to an increasingly sophisticated array of telescopic sights and infra-red image enhancers, its basic design has undergone remarkably little change.

Over any range from four hundred to two thousand metres it is, in the right hands, the most effective way of ensuring the sudden and unexpected death of a single human being since the invention of the cardiac thrombosis.

It is called the Yrscenberg K-11.

As Alanna Kirk swung her car onto the A-59 and accelerated in pursuit of the man who had been named himself in letters to the European media *"El Rey de la Carnicería, Le Roi des Bouchers, Der Gemetzelkönig —* The Slaughter King", an Yrscenberg K-11 was fired on the eastern edge of Edgarhope Wood, a small collection of wind-blasted pine that overlooks the A-697 dual carriageway on the approach to Edinburgh.

A single cupro-titanium jacketed bullet travelled at 1500 metres a second down a hair-thin beam of 20 000 ångström infra-red light.

One-fifteenth of a second after the bullet was fired, it punched a two-centimetre hole in the driver's window of a 1984 light orange Ford station wagon and hit a thirty-two year old woman called Susan Hoffenlight on the head, a centimetre or so behind the right frontozygomstic suture.

Deflected but not stopped by the bone it encountered, it penetrated the brain in the region of the frontal gyrus, travelling diagonally and downwards through the brain tissue until it struck the rear of the skull on the left posterior inferior mastoid angle of the parietal bone.

It bounced again, travelling upwards through the cerebellum, the thalamus, the corpus callosum, until it hit the cranial vault in the region of the parietal foramen.

It then exited through the face.

Unsurprisingly, the woman was dead before it did so.

The Ford station wagon left the road five seconds later.

It rolled three times.

Inside it, centrifugal forces sprayed blood and brain tissue from the massive double wound in the woman's head.

The woman's right arm, sustaining compound fractures of the ulna and radius and carpal bones in doing so, broke the window through which the bullet had entered.

A thin sheaf of papers fell from the glove compartment, whose lock had been broken by the first impact.

The Ford came to rest lying on its roof.

On the eastern edge of Edgarhope Wood, the Yrscenberg K-11 was fired again.

A single cupro-titanium jacketed, lithium-cored bullet travelled at 1500 metres a second down a hair-thin beam of 20 000 ångström infra-red light.

It struck the Ford near the filler cap of the petrol tank, where the deceleration of impact caused the bullet's lithium core to explode at almost the vaporization point of the steel used in the drilling bits of North Sea oil rigs.

4540 degrees centigrade.

An extreme instance of overkill, but effective none the less for it.

The Ford burst into flames.

Convection currents were set up inside the passenger space.

A single page of the sheaf of papers fluttered along the body of the woman towards the smashed window.

Flames invaded the polyoxyliconitrate foam of the padding of the rear passenger seats.

The page fluttered again.

The temperature in the car was rapidly approaching the flash point of the recycled paper that comprised it.

If it had landed on what remained of the woman's face, it would not have come free.

It did not land on what remained of the woman's face.

On the next substantial movement of air within the Ford, it passed through the window and landed on the ground outside the car.

Behind it, the other pages hastened briefly and brightly towards complete carbonization.

Susan Hoffenlight began to cook.

Held in place by the surface tension of a freezing night dew, the page curled and uncurled in the irregular blasts of superheated air pouring from the car.

If anyone had been standing near the page, he or she would have been able to read it easily in the light of the flames.

Had he or she not found the overwhelming smell of charring meat too offensive, of course.

It was covered on one side in neat, hurried handwriting.

An exclamation mark-shaped spot of brain tissue added emphasis to one of the lines.

Towards the bottom of the page, some of the writing was rendered illegible by mud stains from the wet ground:

unnecessarily. The conspiracy involves men and woman at the highest level of both the various national police forces and of their respective governments. I am unable to supply names in detail for any other country than the UK (see final sheet), but links between those involved in this country and those involved overseas will surely be easily traceable.

A consistent component of the conspiracy has been the desire to implicate members of the Goddess-worshipping community in the apparent invulnerability of the King to police investigation. To this end, the King himself has been converted to Goddess worship by, I believe, a mixture of hypnosis and drug treatment. He has almost certainly spent time inside a neurological clinic on mainland Europe, probably the Hans Konig Institute in former East Germany. Instructions have been passed to him by a variety of means, including, as may already have become apparent from the discovery of the one of the King's "bases" in Spain, an electronic device in the base of a Goddess statue, which was triggered by his kneeling before the statue and which I presume could have its messages changed by radio control.

This component of the conspiracy has caused particular distress to myself. I must stress, however, that it was not aimed at me in anything other than an indirect sense. I strongly suspect that the conspiracy has been sponsored by one or more of the extreme Christian evangelical groups in the EC who are seeking to foster an anti-pagan atmosphere by orchestrating the claims of a "satanic" conspiracy. There are also links with the recent "death-squad" scandal in the Metropolitan polic    believe several of those who have resigned from the Govern
        of this are also involved heavily in the Kin            aim of the conspiracy is
to foster an atmo            Pan-European police force can become a seriou
        However, central control of the conspiracy has            believe that at
least one, possibly tw            which it is comprised have had serious
            over the timing of the King's eventu            which his
operations should be conducted.
        As I mentioned briefly above, the Briti            hijacked the conspiracy
entirely. The bringin            been an expedient to the benefit sol
        intended that the King's active            both a distraction from
the election campai            weapon in effect, which the current Ho

# Thirty-Two

Video tape from the forecourt security camera of the overnight petrol station would later be suppressed, somewhat crudely, under a blanket publicity ban.

It would be viewed in a more or less public setting three times before the ban came into effect, twice at Blackburn police headquarters, before its full significance had been realized, and once in London.

The relevant section started with a Fiat swinging off the main road and braking to a halt by the four star petrol pump. A man in his later twenties or early thirties, dressed casually, black-haired, opened the door and got out.

He took the filler cap off the petrol tank of the car. As he lifted the pump handle from the pump, another car swung onto the forecourt from the main road, a Honda hatchback with two people in it.

It braked on the opposite side of the line of petrol pumps, on the left, level with the Fiat. A tall woman in her mid-twenties, dressed in jeans and leather jacket, blonde-haired, got out of the driver's door.

She stepped around the bonnet of her car, holding something in her left hand.

The man was inserting the nozzle of the petrol pump into his Fiat. He glanced back. The woman was standing between two petrol pumps. Her left arm rose. The thing she was carrying was a short-barrelled shotgun. The man threw himself to the ground just before she fired. Pieces of metal flew from the rear of the Fiat.

Very quickly, the man crawled on knees and elbows around the back of his car.

The woman ran out from between the petrol pumps and around the car after him.

On the other side of the car, the man got to his feet and ran to the passenger door. He was opening it as the woman came around the back of the car.

She fired again.

Again, the man didn't seem to be hit.

Through the windscreen of the car, he could be seem throwing himself full-length across the passenger's and driver's seats, tearing at steering wheel and gear-stick.

Swaying, the car accelerated away from the pumps. The nozzle, still inserted in the tank, tore free, spraying petrol and bouncing irregularly on the concrete of the forecourt. The woman was breaking the shotgun's breech and reloading, pulling cartridges from a pocket of her jacket.
The Fiat left the field of the view.
The woman snapped the breech shut and fired, then ran back to her car.
It accelerated very fast, leaving tyre marks on the concrete.
It left the field of view.

# Thirty-Three

On the road about half a kilometre ahead a blue star appeared, blinking on and off and getting nearer very quickly.

There was a turn-off about a fifty metres ahead, on the left.

Alanna made it with about ten seconds to spare.

Parked on the grass verge, she watched through the back window as the police car flew past.

She had lost sight of the King seconds after she left the petrol station in pursuit of him.

The Fiat's engine must have been modified in some way, because it pulled away from the Honda travelling at nearly one hundred and twenty kilometres as though it were *poured* forward into the darkness like blood or oil.

A last glimpse of red tail-lights, tiny as embers, then nothing.

She swore, and Sansiega, half-unconscious in the passenger seat, stirred and half-lifted both hands towards the windscreen.

A second later the police car had appeared ahead of them.

Now she sat, thinking.

She reached into the back seat for the pad and a pen.

Wrote on the pad.

Held it in front of Sansiega.

— Where will he be?

Sansiega shook her head.

— THINK! It has to be the end for him now. Where will he go? Use the book.

Sansiega held out her hand for the pen. Alanna gave it to her. She wrote.

— Don't know. He *utiliza* the book not always. Don't know. Let me sleep.

Alanna took hold of her by the chin and turned her face towards herself. With her other hand she took hold of the lobe of her left ear between the

150

nails of forefinger and thumb and pinched.

Sansiega screamed.

Alanna let go of her chin and slapped her.

She released the ear lobe.

Blood streamed thinly from it.

The tips of Alanna's fingers were red with it.

She picked up the pad and indicated a line, leaving a smear of blood on the paper.

— THINK! It has to be the end for him now. Where will he go? Use the book.

Sansiega shook her head slowly. Tears were beginning to leak from her eyes. She cupped her wounded ear. Blood leaked slowly between her fingers.

Alanna slapped her again, shouting.

Sansiega squeezed herself back in her seat, towards the door.

As Alanna tried to slap her again, she put up her hand to ward off the blow.

Alanna grabbed her by the wrist and twisted it.

She put her mouth down to the hand.

Sansiega squeezed the hand into a fist.

Alanna bit the knuckle of the little finger.

She lifted her head, licking her lips, twisting the wrist harder.

Sansiega's face glistened with thin planes of tears.

She was nodding, shouting something.

Alanna let go of her wrist and picked up the pad and pen from where they had fallen to the floor.

Sansiega wrote.

— *arboleda de manzanas*

Alanna read the words. She shook her head, lifting her eyebrows.

Sansiega wrote again.

— *arboleda* = place of *arboles*. *manzana es fruto*.

Alanna put her finger on *"arboles"*, shaking her head.

Sansiega drew a picture of a tree.

Alanna stared at the pad.

She opened the door of the car and got out.

There were houses on either side of the road, behind hedges or low walls. She went to the nearest, running up the driveway and into the porch, pressing the bell hard several times.

After thirty seconds or so the frosted glass panels in the door went bright as a light was switched on inside the house.

Alanna had pulled out her wallet and taken out her ID card.

The shape of man loomed through the glass.

A chain rattled.

The door swung open half a metre, leashed on a security chain.

An old man's head half-appeared around it, pink and balding.

A pyjama collar hung stiffly under his chin.

He blinked at her, scowling a little.

"Who the foock are you?"

She held up the card.

"Police. I'm very sorry to disturb you but I need some information, very urgently."

The old man pursed his lips, looking at the card.

He didn't unhook the security chain.

"What you want to know?"

"Do you know of any apple orchards around here?"

"What?"

"Apple orchards. Any sort of orchard."

"What sort of daft question is that? Are you trying to booger me about or sommat? If y'are, you can just piss off."

"I'm sorry, but I'm very serious. I'm very sorry to disturb you, Mr..?"

"Heaton."

"I'm very sorry, Mr Heaton, but I can assure you I'm very serious."

He stared at her face.

"Alreet. I'm thinking. Wait. I'll go and ask me wife. She does gardening, not me."

His head left the gap and she saw him walking away from the door.

She tried to control her impatience but it was impossible.

The old man's shape loomed on the glass again.

His head appeared.

"The only place she know round 'ere where there's owt like what you want is up Barton Grange. The nurseries. There's everything there. Apple trees, the lot."

"Where is it?"

"On't A6. Follow't main road that way" — he jerked his head to indicate

— "into Preston. You coom across A6, tek it north. Keep an eye out and you shouldn't miss it."

Already running back for the car, she called, "Mr Heaton, thank you. Thank you!"

# Thirty-Four

He drove between the greenhouses, head turning quickly left-right. They were full of dark shapes, looming shapes, half-vegetable, half, it seemed, animal. On the panes of one, as he passed it, there was a sudden dull glittering, and his hands tightened on the wheel for a moment in surprise before he realized that an automatic sprinkler was working inside.

He was beyond the greenhouses: ahead of him now was a series of buildings and long sheds, and a long concrete space divided at one end by white strips into parking spacing.

There was a car parked by the first building, an old Morris, and a window down one end of the building, at the opposite corner, bled yellow light into the darkness. Moths spiralled in and out of the light, bouncing on the glass of the window.

He stopped the car and sat for a moment staring towards the light.

He got out.

The car was ticking slowly with fatigue.

He rested his hand on the bonnet. The metal was hot, very hot, and after a second it hurt him to keep his hand there. He held it in place a second, two, three, longer, and then walked towards the light.

There was a door at the near corner of the building. He tested the handle. It was stiff, and for a moment he thought it was locked, and then, creaking a little, it turned, and he could pull the door open.

He stepped through. On the other side there was a small space, not really a room, not really a corridor. There were boxes piled along the wall to his left, stationery boxes, paper, folders, pads; on the wall on the right there were posters, diagrams of plants marked with the bright discolorations of disease, safety information posters with red-crossed boxes on one side showing cartoon figures lifting heavy weights incorrectly or slipping on oil-soaked workshop floors, and blue-ticked boxes on the other side with the situations rectified; in the wall ahead of him there was a counter and a sliding window of frosted glass, closed. The window was brightly lit.

He walked forward.

Next to the counter, on the right, there was a doorway.

He walked through it.

There was a room on the other side of it, dimly lit by light coming through a doorway leading to the room on the other side of the frosted glass. He walked to the doorway and looked in.

The light was coming from two fluorescent tubes in the ceiling of a square room full of computer equipment — screens, keyboards, printers. A man was sitting, back to the door, in front of one of the computers, typing. He was black-haired, young-looking, wearing jeans and a white T-shirt, neither very clean-looking. The headphones of a personal stereo were clamped on his head. They hissed loudly over the clatter of the keyboard and the man's head was shaking faintly, as though in time to music.

The King relaxed and stepped into the room, standing directly behind the man so that his reflection would not appear on the screen of the computer. He pulled out his knife and stepped forward again to stand directly behind the man.

He was finding it hard not to laugh.

He held the knife out and reached out with his other hand for the headphones.

It would have to be done in the same second.

THe same split-second.

Go!

He hooked the headphones off and pushed the tip of the knife into the man's back, hard but not too hard, barely cutting through the T-shirt. With a wheeze of surprise, the man stiffened.

"If you move, I'll kill you."

He could hear the music from the earphones now, tinny but distinct, sounding very loud in the stillness.

He didn't recognize it. It sounded like shit to him.

"Turn the music off," he said.

Very slowly, the man reached for something on his lap. There was a click and the music stopped.

"Thank you."

He waited a little while, enjoying himself, and then pushed the knife very slowly into the man's back.

Into the vertebral border of the right scapula, *más o menos*.

A spot of red appeared on the T-shirt.

After a second or so, another appeared where the T-shirt was tucked into the waistband of the jeans.

He watched them widen.

The man was trembling with pain, very faintly.

He withdrew the knife.

Pushed it slowly through the T-shirt in a new place.
The left teres major.
Another red spot, widening.
The man sobbed once, quietly.
He withdrew the knife.
Over the vertebrae, this time, *¿qué piensas?*
The fourth thoracic, you say?
The fourth thoracic.
He watched the spot of red widen like a flower.
Shifted his feet on the floor.
Put both of his hands to the haft of the knife.
Slowly inhaled.
Very quickly and suddenly shoved the knife into the spinal column.
There was a sharp wet rasp of metal on bone, and the man toppled sideways, one hand flapping and flailing at the computer for support.
The knife jerked in the King's hands as though it were trying to drag itself free.
The man's head hit the top of the computer desk and he stopped falling sideways.
Something bubbled inside his throat.
As he died, he tried to say something.
Didn't manage it.
Thick liquid splattered inside his jeans.
The King's nostrils flared reflexively on a stench of faeces.
He tightened his grip and pulled the knife out.
It glistened with blood and synovial fluid.
He wiped against the man's back.
The dead right hand had come to rest on the keyboard.
The King looked at the screen to see what it had typed.

# Thirty-Five

Ahead of her, gleaming like bone in the headlights, Alanna saw the gate-bar.

It had been lifted aside.

He was here.

She switched off the headlights and drove through the gate.

The road curved ahead of her, faintly darker between the jumbled shapes of the earth and trees on either side.

She drove slowly, straining her eyes ahead.

Beside her, unheard, Sansiega poured words in an ecstacy of pain, rocking in her seat, hand cupped to her ear, hand fisted to her mouth. Her seatbelt loosened and tautened, snapping to the rhythm of her movements. She heard it as the flapping of wide wings in the sky above. She smiled and spoke to them, firing words like arrows of fire into the dark wind-wounded vault.

Spanish trailed phoenix feathers of flame, gold-dusted purple woven with the bright bubbling scarlet of the blood of Talmudic scholars.

English, sea-wine blues, the whites of speaking sails, soot-darkened greens.

Basque, witch-wing blacks, the dancing yellows-on-reds of herb-sprinkled embers, rain-plump forest colours.

Fleshless, she smiled.

Her breath sang, stinking sweetly.

Her words were wax birds, birthed by her throat, moulded by the hot tissues of her moving mouth and lips, nipped off short by her teeth,

They fluttered inside the car, smelling of ecclesiastical Latin.

Wide wings beat in the sky above her.

Gem-clogged bowels were loosed upon them, the vivid dung pattering softly on the windows and roof like rain.

Alanna switched on the windscreen wipers with a Kalahari click of irritation.

The car came around the corner, and ahead of her, dimly in the light of approaching dawn, she saw the greenhouses and bedding rows, plants hunched low to the earth or rising against the sky for acres.

From the far side of the buildings an eye of round water, pale with the sky's reflex, stared at her, foreshortened to narrow oval.

The car passed between the first greenhouses.

They were full of looming shapes, blind leaf-mouthed nymphs, patient in the sleep-imposing darkness, dreaming of the sun's rising, the pouring upon them of her benedictant golden piss.

She saw a dull glittering of water on the panes of one of the greenhouses.

As the car passed the greenhouse, the glittering stopped.

She saw the buildings ahead of her, the two cars, and the moth-busy wound of yellow light.

She stopped the car and picked up the shotgun from beneath her feet.

Opened the door and climbed out, clicking the central locking on.

Drizzle spotted her face with cold.

A shadow of decay flickered in the wound of light.

She ran towards the open door, locking the gun in her hands, its short iron mouth pointing ahead of her.

Inside the building the King ran, unbelieving.

She passed through the door, through the storeroom and turned as the King had done.

She looked through the doorway into the lit room, smelling death before she saw it, and ran down the dark corridor ahead of her, knowing he fled her.

The light wood of the floor sprang and resounded under her feet.

A tall shape loomed and she fired without thought.

The pellets clanged and crashed unheard against a filing cabinet, but the darkness had leapt back a little on the stab of light from the gun's nozzle, and she had seen a worm of movement twisting for a second a few metres ahead of her.

When she reached the spot she found a door swinging on the outside darkness.

She kicked it fully open, cracking the breech of the shotgun and pulling the used cartridge out with her injured hand, enjoying the pain of moving it in the ecstacy of the hunt.

The cartridge seared her fingers.

She pushed a fresh one into the gun and snapped it shut.

She ran out.

On her left, and behind her, was the concrete space on which the cars were parked.

Directly ahead of her lay a long open shed. She could dimly see long trestles inside the shed, covered in plant pots. White labels hung against the black shapes of plants like sleep-dimmed eyes.

She stopped.

He was there.

She could smell him.

Choked in silence, her four senses hunted the darkness like hounds.

He was there.

She could smell him.

She walked forward.

He was there.

She could smell him.

She called.

"Sansiega! The car! Give me light!"

Over and over.

She looked back.

The cars lay dead.

"Sansiega! Give me light!"

Light swept over her.

She looked back.

The headlamps of the Honda blazed.

The passenger door opened out like a wing and Sansiega climbed out.

"No! Stay in the fucking car!"

Alanna snapped her head round, back to the shed.

It was full of light.

On the back wall, the shadows of plants stood like saw-toothed blades.

She smelt Sansiega's sweat, and she was standing beside her, staring into the shed.

The King stepped from the shed.

A long knife shone in his hand like a leaf of ice.

His face was round and radiated madness like a sun.

She pointed the shotgun at his throat.

"Do you understand English? Nod if you do."

He nodded.

Sun-set, sun-rise.

His lips moved.

"Don't speak. Throw your knife to me."

Beside her, Sansiega moved.

In the sky above, a black swan squawked like thunder.

The wide wings beat once more and were still.

The King was a man-tall flower, opening petals long as swords thirstily to the sky.

Blood poured into him, steaming.

"Throw your knife to me."
Blood filled the flower and overran it, splattering to the ground.
The blood-steam thickened.
The petals of the flower closed.
They were transparent, like glass.
In the blood, a foetus hung, veined with fire.
The foetus's mouth moved, calling her.
She started to walk to it.
Alanna fired.
The King was too quick, almost.
A triangular chunk had been taken from his shoulder.
The curves of the scapula and the head of the humerus showed white
through shredded muscle.
Blood spurted.
Alanna swung the gun to him again, but as it drew level again with his
throat he had gathered Sansiega to himself with his knife arm, swinging
her to shield his body.
A liquid flower of blood danced on his broken shoulder.
The ice blade of the knife was at Sansiega's throat.
He smiled, face webbed tightly with pain.
She fired the gun.
A wide mouth opened on Sansiega's chest, barred with horizontal white.
She snapped the gun open, fed more cartridges into it.
Fired it again into the wide, babbling mouth.
Again.
Carving her way through the shield.
In the curve of the King's arm, the body had gone limp.
As she fired, it thudded backwards against him.
He began to walk backwards, dragging it with him, shouting.
She walked after him, reloading.

# *Epilogue*

Saphique put down the phone and went over to the stereo. The cassette was still where she had hidden it. She pulled it out, opened it.

Five minutes of playing time left.

Nothing of life.

She pushed it into the stereo and pressed PLAY.

When the *Dysmenorrhoea* had hammered at last into silence on the speakers, she loosened the clenching of her hands, slowly, almost having to persuade the muscles to obey her. First, the right: and she held the palm flat out in front of her, staring down into it as though she would read something there in the lines and creases and the four moon-shaped marks of her fingernails; then, the left: and again she stared down into the palm held out flat in front of her beside her right hand, and whether she read anything there or did not, nothing in her face revealed.

At last she lowered the palms flat to the floor and lifted her knees up onto them and leaned her weight forward into them, grinding them down into the carpet. She lifted her head back and looked up the ceiling, shook her head from side to side, looked down again. Her lips began to work, silently, repeating a single word over and over again until she bit down on them, to poison their independence with pain and still them. Then, looking down, she closed her eyes.

Some time later, she opened them again. When she took her hands from beneath her knees and stood up, she could not feel them. She had crushed all sensation out of them and she could only be sure that she could still move them by watching them. They seemed like white, dead little creatures on the ends of her arms, cold, dead little creatures grafted to her sometime while she had slept.

First, she took them with her to the telephone, emptying all her credit cards from her handbag. She spoke quietly and quickly for several minutes. All the time, as she spoke, she was opening and closing her hands, working life back into them and knowing the return of life by the pain each began to give her.

Then, the calls made, she carried the hands through to the bathrooms of the house, where they worked stiffly for her, plugging sinks and baths and spinning taps for her. After a time water, like faint, far-off lionesses, was crashing and roaring everywhere as the baths and sinks began to fill.

Moments after she had visited the last bathroom, the bell of the gate chimed.

Sleeves rolled up on her elbows, she walked quickly through to the sitting room. Looking down into the street, she saw the first of the delivery vans pull up alongside the kerb, and even as she left the window to open the door, a second and third slid into place behind it.

After this, she kept the front door open and the delivery men came in a steady stream, each depositing his load to her few words of command and then leaving. When the last had left she closed the front door and began to seal the house off from the outside world, unhooking all the phones, unplugging the televisions and video and microwave, closing all the windows, locking the doors.

This done, she walked through to her bedroom, undressed and, naked, carried back to the living room an inflatable, inflated chair made of transparent plastic and shaped like the half-open shell of a scallop. Already, as she did this, she could see, beneath the steam billowing from the bathroom doors, clear, irregular fingers of water reaching out across the thresholds for the rest of the house, and as she laid the chair in the space reserved for it on the Chinese carpet and went to fetch a small ceremonial knife from the altar, a first finger was poking through into the living room.

When she came back with the knife, the finger had thickened and its tip had already vanished into the carpet of white flowers and green leaves with which the floor was now almost completely covered. She walked back to the chair and sat down, resting the knife across her thighs, the metal of the blade cool upon the left, the polished wooden handle smooth upon the right. Then, with her feet planted firmly to the floor, she waited for the water to rise around her.

And gradually, from its steaming wombs in the thunderous bathrooms,. it did, running into the living room first in finger's-breaths and then wide streams and then a steady steaming sheet filling the doorway from jamb to jamb, rising invisibly at first beneath the flowers and leaves, its presence signalled only in shiftings and jerkings of the green-white carpet, a restless movement of stems and leaves and flowers that vibrated unevenly as though small animals were burrowing everywhere beneath them.

Steam began to fill the air, rising up between Saphique and the huge vague shapes of the television and phone table and the room's other furniture, around which the men had woven the flowers at her direction, and the water began to rise across her feet, warm, like smooth skin. She

162

smiled, looking around her at the white flowers. Their scent was heavy enough, almost, to drug her: a pure, warm smell, like the smell of molten wax.

The water was around her ankles now and she lifted her feet, taking hold of the little knife lest it should fall, and, tucking her wet soles up underneath her, laid it across her lap. The steam was thicker and she felt her hair shift faintly, tugging here and there on her scalp as it absorbed the air's moisture; and on the smooth plastic of the chair droplets of water were condensing.

She stirred at these idly with a forefinger, joining two small drops, three, four, five into a larger that suddenly ran away from the finger down the curve of the chair to the rising water, almost as though the motion of her finger had caused the chair pain, and the droplet had been a tear.

A flower bobbed up suddenly from the floral carpeting in front of her, then toppled sideways on its sisters: the water was beginning to lift the flowers clear of the floor. She shifted herself on the chair, finding a balance for her limbs and torso against the time when the water would begin to lift the chair too, up amongst the floating flowers, whose scent had begun to lessen, weakened in reality perhaps, by the steam, or in perception, by her familiarity with it.

She drew deeply on the air, releasing it in long hisses through a slotted mouth, but the scent was fading, yes, in reality or in perception. More of the flowers were floating now, more beginning to drift on the rising surface of the water, turning, locking together, stem to stem, leaf to leaf, forming rafts that themselves turned on the water, gathering more flowers to themselves, flower galaxies that spun and bumped gently against the sides of the chair in which Saphique sat waiting to be lifted and turned on the water herself.

She lifted her arms up and wide, dipping them on either side into the water, as though to awaken it. And yes, the chair trembled: the water was shin-high, rising, and all the flowers that had been laid upon the floor were floating: soon, the chair would lift free to join them. The water's surface steamed thinly but beneath it, between the flower-rafts, through the transparent plastic of the chair visible around and between her thighs, even, the water was very clear and she could see the pattern of the carpet almost perfectly. Suddenly the chair jerked, trembled for a moment; and then, the chair bobbing a little for a moment or two beneath her, she was afloat.

Carefully, she dabbed at the water with her hands and the chair began to turn amongst the flowers, slowly. She tilted her head back until she felt the water begin to soak her hair, back a little further, then slowly and carefully unfolded her legs and lifted them forward and down into the warm water and the sharp tickling of the leaves and stems, the softness of the white petals.

When she felt the beetle run from a flower onto her foot she closed her mouth, opened her eyes and looked down. It was resting on her left ankle, its long antennae twiddling interrogatively and, she thought, somewhat doubtfully. It was a small, slim beetle, with legs and antennae almost as long as its body; small-headed, black-pronotum'd, with yellow, black-banded wing-covers; as she watched it, it seemed to reach a decision and began to run up her leg with great dexterity and speed.

A week before the tickling of its minute, busy feet on her skin would have brought her to a near hysteria of disgust; now, as it swayed a second on the summit of her knees and then ran quickly down between her thighs, she giggled, and held back greater mirth, for fear that it would be frightened or shaken from her body, and she wanted to see how it would deal with the thousand soft snares of her pubes.

Thinking this, she plucked the knife from her lap and watched as the beetle ran until, travelling too quickly down the smooth precipice of her inner thighs to turn aside, it rushed in amongst her pubic hairs and was snagged. She watched it struggle, fight free and be caught again, deeper within the hairs, struggle, fight free again, struggle on, rising and falling amongst the curls, hidden and half-hidden from view as though it were a ship or swimmer striving against the black turbulence of a whirlpool, or against the thousand tentacles of a kraken risen from the smooth-throated submarine cavern of her vagina.

Smiling at these conceits, she watched it fight to the centre of her pubes, where again, as on her foot, it stopped, turning its antennae to and fro, as though it wondered to itself how it had come to find itself in its predicament.

Then, like little knife-covers flicked back, it swung its elytra wide from its delicate wings and sprung into the air. It was difficult to follow the quick curve of its flight in the steam: she thought perhaps it had landed on the mass of lilies around the television, or perhaps merely flown near this, and landed on the wall. But it did not matter where it was: she could not see it anyway; and there was nothing to hold her attention now; and the knife was in her hand.

She smiled again, kicking her feet in the water and leaning her head back again to the ceiling, and closed her eyes again, and held the knife in her left hand and brought her right hand across and turned the wrist towards the ceiling, bending the hand back to tighten the skin.

For a moment she did nothing, imagining behind closed eyelids the smooth, uncut skin, and then she dropped the knife to the wrist, moved it a little across and towards the hand, and drew it deep across the smooth, vein-traced throat of the wrist.

The knife was very sharp and the cut burned fiercely, but not like fire, like ice, and it seemed strange to feel that the liquid was warm that spilled from it and flowed down her arm as she swapped the knife from the murdering left hand into the murdered right, and laid the left hand down with wrist turned to the ceiling, and swung the knife over and touched it to the skin, adjusted it, and drew the knife across deeply for the second time.

Now she opened her eyes and held her arms up, smiling to see the fountaining throats, and the bright glint of the knife that had bitten them out for her, and the blood that heightened the white of her skin with its red, running warmly and smoothly everywhere.

She flung the knife sideways and it clunked against a wall and fell *sclish!* into the water. But she did not hear it, for the blood pouring from her wrists held her fascinated. She squeezed together her thighs and sucked in her belly and poured blood into the cup so formed at the intersection of belly and thighs, holding the wrists together so that the blood-streams mingled; and when her pubes was drowned in a bright triangle of blood she brought the wrists apart and up her body, pouring blood across her breasts and shoulders and, turning her wrists side to side to side, her face and head; and finally, with blood running everywhere upon her body and streaming smoothly from the plastic of the scallop-chair into the water, she lifted her arms high and shook and threw them up and across and round, aspergilling the steam-filled air and the water and the floating lilies, many of which caught the blood on their white lips and swallowed it, deep into their scented throats.

Shortly, she felt weaker, and brought her arms down and held them wide, dangling her wrists amongst the flowers and in the water, watching sleepily as the blood streamed and ran for what seemed to her hours, slow red streams turning and twisting and fading away into the clear warm water.

*The*
# CREATION
*Publishing Group*

# BAD BLOOD
## *Transgressive Art & Literature*

---

**"THE SLAUGHTER KING"** Simon Whitechapel           *Bad Blood 1*
A sadistic serial killer is leaving a seemingly random trail of butchered corpses, both male and female, across Europe. He kills and mutilates with the skill and anatomical precision of a surgeon, the flair of a surrealist painter, the insatiable ferocity of a beast. *El Rey.* The Slaughter King.
With only the help of the dying girl who alone holds the key to the slaughter, policewoman Alanna Kirk trails this psychopathic destroyer from Northern Spain through a dark underworld of S&M sex, organized suicide and police corruption, to the industrial North of England — only to find that there are those who want the Slaughter King very much alive and on the streets...
*"Whitechapel is one of the new breed of crime writers, ready to slice through narrative as easily as slicing through flesh. It's about time that the crime genre was infected by the blood of these people, intent on dragging its razored corpse into the age of AIDS, the Serial Killer and end-of-millennium sexual psychosis."*
— PAUL BUCK (Author, "The Honeymoon Killers")
**£7.95**


**"SEX MURDER ART"** — The Films of Jörg Buttgereit     *Bad Blood 2*
HEADPRESS co-editor David Kerekes has produced the definitive book on the controversial young German director whose films, such as **NEKROMANTIK, NEKROMANTIK 2**, and **DER TODESKING** have already earned him a reputation as one of the most original, innovative and *dangerous* of all modern film-makers. Buttgereit's films deal explicitly with death, and feature graphic images of necrophilia, grave-robbing, murder and suicide.
The author uses detailed analysis of all the films, dozens of rare and often disturbing photographs, plus extensive personal interviews with not only Buttgereit but also his principal players, to create a comprehensive and illuminating study: possibly the ultimate testament to the obsession, paranoia and politics of modern underground film-making.
**"SEX MURDER ART"** is published to coincide with the British première of Buttgereit's new film **SCHRAMM**.
*"DER TODESKING is the first truly post-modern horror film."*
— RAMSEY CAMPBELL
**£9.95**

**"HEADPRESS ONE"** — **The Best of Headpress Magazine**    *Bad Blood 3*
The very best articles, interviews and photographs from HEADPRESS — the
magazine of Sex, Religion & Death — whose early issues are already notorious,
long-deleted collectors' items.
**HEADPRESS ONE** will feature a wide range of subjects, including bizarre
sexual activities, weird crime cases, underground performance artists, writers and
film-makers, religious manias and fanaticism, and many other little-covered or
misrepresented facets of "apocalypse culture". Interviewees range from porno
queen Annie Sprinkle, through body-piercer Patrick to film director Alejandro
Jodorowski, plus dozens of other unrepentant characters.
The book will be illustrated throughout with rare photographs and artworks.
*"Particularly bizarre ... disturbing and sometimes delightful."* — **TIME OUT**
*"Remarkable ... one of the most most turbo-charged publications to appear in
mnan a month."* — **DARK SIDE**
*"An entirely healthy interest in violent death and deviant sex."* - **i-D**
**£9.95**

# ANNIHILATION
### Cinema, Art, Music, True Crime, Occult

## RAPID EYE

*RAPID EYE is the much-acclaimed "Occulture" journal, probably the only professionally-published British book which comprehensively explores the dark side of our popular culture, and examines the way society is really reacting to the coming end-of-millennium crises. Through its wide-ranging articles, which deal with subjects from Control and Conspiracy, Underground Art, Literature, Music and Film, to the Occult, Body Art, Psychopharmacology, Serial Killers, Virtual Reality, and everything between, RAPID EYE discloses a global society of inter-connected chaos, confronts this occult (hidden) network and both offers and encourages a real response to it.*
*RAPID EYE is a truly post-Modern phenomenon. While most of today's art and media describe appearance, RAPID EYE describes reality.*

## RAPID EYE 1 *New and Revised Edition*
### Simon Dwyer (Editor)
WILLIAM S. BURROUGHS * BRION GYSIN * KATHY ACKER * ALEISTER CROWLEY
THEE TEMPLE OF PSYCHIC YOUTH * DEREK JARMAN * COLIN WILSON
CHARLES MANSON * HUBERT SELBY Jr * JIM JONES * AUSTIN SPARE
TATTOOS & PIERCING * ALCHEMY * COSMOLOGY * NEOISM * MESCALIN
DREAMACHINE * HITLER UFOs * KENNEDY CONSPIRACY
*and much more...*
*496 pages  A5  Illustrated*                                    **£11.95**

## RAPID EYE 2 Simon Dwyer (Editor)
JÖRG BUTTGEREIT * RICHARD KERN * GENESIS P-ORRIDGE * ANTON LAVEY
PAUL MAYERSBERG * VICTOR BOCKRIS * THE OTHER BISEXUALITY
MONDO MOVIES * TIMOTHY LEARY * TWILIGHT LANGUAGE * CIA
COLIN WILSON * ALEX SANDERS * KENNETH ANGER * SAVOY BOOKS
H.P. LOVECRAFT * LOBSANG RAMPA * AARON WILLIAMSON * JEFF KOONS
*and much more...*
*400 pages  A5  Illustrated*                                    **£9.95**

*"...RAPID EYE tells you what is really happening. It tells a wider story of a cultural struggle that will be crucial to the demands of the 90's:  the struggle between life and death."* — **THE OBSERVER**
*"To read RAPID EYE is to descend into chaos ... This is the first and final battle."* — **MELODY MAKER**
*"Guaranteed to blow your mind. Utterly essential."* — **OUTLOOK**

# CREATION

## *Imaginative Extremes in Fiction & Poetry*

**"SATANSKIN"   James Havoc**
Twenty adult fairy-tales of twisted imagination from the young "madman", disclosing an occult world of graveyard erotica, faecal demonolatry, magick and pansexual lunar mutiny.
In *Devil's Gold*, a transexual pact with excremental demons leads to unexpected metamorphoses; the sorcerer of *White Meat Fever* steals female anatomy to usurp the moon; skinless nuns with *Shadow Sickness* fall prey to a priapic scavenger from Hell; a hapless traveller enters the *Tongue Cathedral* and finds himself inside a vampire's wet-dream; in *The Venus Eye*, an angel wreaks revenge on a paedophiliac butcher from within her coffin; at the throw of bone dice, the *Dogstar Pact* induces lycanthropy in unborn children...
*"As a literary bestiary of gratuitous sexual horrors, SATANSKIN is up there with 120 Days of Sodom, genuinely infernal and black."* — DIVINITY
*"SATANSKIN is a journal conceived in madness and typed upon the hide of its victims"* — HELLRAISER
**£5.95**

**"RAISM - The Songs of Gilles de Rais"   James Havoc and Mike Philbin**
**Part I: "Meathook Seed"**
Havoc's infamous anti-novel, heavily edited and revised to form a graphic novel in 3 parts, plus a brand new fourth and concluding part. Illustrated in finepoint chiaroscuro by Mike Philbin of **"Red Hedz"** notoriety. A surreal, explicit, and deranged work of alchemy and Satanism, unlike any other of its kind.
*"...bursting with darkly imaginative, not to say downright revolting, imagery."*
— DARKSIDE
*Creation Graphics 1*   A4, 32 pages. Full colour cover.
**£4.95**

**"RED HEDZ"   Michael Paul Peter**
The hardcore horror classic; an extreme onslaught of shape-shifting, psycho-sexual tyranny and mutation.
*"Horror fiction on the edge."* — RAMSEY CAMPBELL
*"Would make a perfect David Cronenberg film if translated to the screen."*
— JÖRG BUTTGEREIT
*"...takes writers like William Burroughs and Clive Barker as merely the starting-point for a mixture of poetry, cut-up fiction, hallucinatory rantings and keenly-observed characterisation."* — SKELETON CREW
**£5.95**

**"THE BLACK BOOK"   Tony Reed (Ed.)**
The sex and death show.
A disturbing collection of urban horror and psycho-sexual derangement by new
writers and illustrators presenting their own personal vision of Hell.
*"Genuinely painful and worth investigating"* — **i-D**
**£4.95**

**"RED STAINS"   Jack Hunter (Ed.)**
A lexicon of lesions, bible of blood.
New stories of extreme biological fantasy and the psycho-sexual imagination. A
successor to the **"Black Book"**. Authors include: **Ramsey Campbell, Jeremy
Reed, Tony Reed, Terence Sellers, James Havoc, Paul Buck, DF Lewis,
Michael Paul Peter Philbin, Adèle Olivia Gladwell.**
*"The most unrelenting collection of sexual horror fiction that I've ever read."*
— **DIVINITY**
**£5.95**

**"KICKS"   Jeremy Reed**
A brand new collection of poems, short erotic film-scripts and prose-pieces, from
"the most imaginatively gifted poet since Dylan Thomas" (— *Kathleen Raine*).
Kicks features the most outrageous, sexually outspoken side of Jeremy Reed.
*"A brilliant and original talent"* — **J.G. BALLARD**
**£7.95**

**"CATHEDRAL LUNG"   Aaron Williamson**
A volume of ecstatic rage from the explosive writer and performer, who is
profoundly deaf.
*"Aaron seems to confront his anger by grabbing language by the throat...creates
something radically different from most writers."* — **SOUNDBARRIER**
*"...a furious gnostic prayer...machine-gunning the page, ricocheting against our
smug complacent ears."* — **BRIAN CATLING**
**£4.95**

**"A HOLYTHROAT SYMPOSIUM"   Aaron Williamson**
The assembled 'acts of writing' orbit the poet's deafness with a static insistency;
an explosive poetry surfaces, squalling, devouring the pages. Williamson has
burdened his work with the weight of the physical world; at the heart of the book
is an unspeakable surdity, a silent flickering language ravenous for release,
possessing any and every faculty: a primal world of violence and estrangement
of one who is 'anatomically exiled' from the language he uses. A Holythroat
Symposium is vertiginously layered, accumulating a physical impact; an irritant
compulsion contorting its anatomical intelligence.
*"A merciless winnowing to gist. Savage in rhetoric. Farctate. Exploring all the
dark resources of fault."* — **IAIN SINCLAIR**
**£7.95**

## "INTERREGNUM"   Geraldine Monk

In 1612, ten people from the Pendle area of East Lancashire were hanged as witches in the city of Lancaster. Unquestionably, they fell victim to a *language-magic* far more powerful and effective than their own: the language-magic possessed by, and misused by, the governing authorities, rendering the witches' magic meaningless. A state of interregnum was created, whereby accepted codings no longer applied and the relationship between words and actions became completely arbitrary. Contemporary and historical abuse and misuse of language-magic, which determines degrees of freedom, is the recurring theme in the text of **Interregnum**, and culminates in the nemesis of the witches' monologues.

*"Parallel texts, image chains, ikon-like symmetrical designs are all animated by Monk's special willingness to submerge herself completely into her experience."*
— **THE GUARDIAN**

£7.95

## "THE RISEN"   Peter Whitehead

Sexual magick, Shamanism, crystallography, Egyptology, Virtual Reality, psychopharmacology, Grail mythology — author Peter Whitehead has taken themes and images from all of these and more, to produce an authentic picture of the transformed consciousness mankind will need to adopt in the not too distant future. Two truth-seekers conduct seemingly unconnected, simultaneous experiments — one splitting a pyramid-shaped diamond with X-ray lasers, the other splitting his mind by ingesting a crystalline psychedelic drug. Their parallel researches are destined to lead them to the only conceivable meeting-point — infinity. **The Risen** charts their collision course through a labyrinth of disturbing eroticism, dismemberment and reincarnation, drawing the reader through the half-silvered mirror of reason into its own time-space, a virtual inscape fusing magical imagery from holography and morphic resonance, fetishistic sex and pagan initiation rites: an occult *tour-de-force* which may well alter our perception of reality — forever.

PETER WHITEHEAD is the former 60's *avant-garde* film-maker and Rolling Stones documentarist.

*"This highly original work may well be the future of the novel"*
— **ANDREW SINCLAIR**

£8.95

## "BRIDAL GOWN SHROUD"   Adèle Olivia Gladwell

Short fiction, prose-poems and illuminating essays dealing with sexual/textual politics. Using a subversive motif of menstruation, the writer explores the gulf between the symbolic and the imaginary to comment upon the abjection and fragmentation of the misplaced woman. Includes essays on Nick Cave, Religious Ecstasy, Pornography etc.

*"The missing link between Lydia Lunch and Julia Kristeva."* — **LOADED**
*"Compelling, strangely addictive...violent images of sex and blood."*
— **OUTLOOK**

£6.95

**"THE HAUNTED PALACE"**   Edgar Allan Poe        *Creation Classics I*
*Death Poems & Vampire Tales*
The quintessence of Poe's artistic vision: a body of obsessive work which stands as one of the great testaments to the inseparable passions of love and death. As well as his darkest poetry, this new, revised edition contains the "vampire" cycle of 5 stories which in many ways forms the nucleus of his prose work. In these stories Poe investigates the vampiric nature of human relationships, including love and lust both "normal" and incestuous, and develops his theme to observe the vampiric qualities inherent in the creative or artistic process.
The texts are accompanied by lithographs by the 19th century Symbolist **Odilon Redon**, taken from his series dedicated to Poe in 1882.
**£7.95**

**"PHILOSOPHY IN THE BOUDOIR"**   De Sade        *Creation Classics II*
Probably the single most representative (and concise) text out of all the Marquis de Sade's works, containing all his libertine doctrines expounded in full, as well as liberal doses of the unbridled eroticism for which he is (unfairly) more renowned. The renegade philosophies put forward here are amongst the main cornerstones of the Surrealist manifesto.
This seminal text is here presented in a *brand new*, modern and authentic translation by Meredith Bodroghy, herself a former dominatrix descended of Hungarian aristocracy. Second, revised edition.
**£7.95**

**"BLOOD AND ROSES"**                        *Creation Classics III*
**Edited by James Havoc and Adèle Olivia Gladwell**
An anthology of 19th century literature in which the vampire appears as a metaphor for erotic delirium, menstruation etc. Translators old and new include Lafcadio Hearn, Alexis Lykiard and Jeremy Reed.
Authors include: **Poe, Lautréamont, Gautier, Oscar Wilde, Huysmans, Baudelaire, Bram Stoker, Sheridan le Fanu** and many others. Possibly the definitive book on its subject. Illustrated throughout with the Satanic/Erotic works of Felicien Rops.
*"As near to definitive as anyone's ever got"* — MELODY MAKER
**£7.95**

**"CRAWLING CHAOS"**   H. P. Lovecraft        *Creation Classics IV*
At last, a quality single edition of the best works of Lovecraft. Contains 23 stories, prose-poems and collaborative pieces from 1920 to 1935, including several unusual items. With a brand new introduction by Colin Wilson. *368 pages, large de-luxe format.*
**£9.95**

**"THE GREAT GOD PAN"**　Arthur Machen　　　　　*Creation Classics V*
First published in 1894, *THE GREAT GOD PAN* is Arthur Machen's first, and greatest, opus of Decadence and Horror. With his singular eye for the bizarre and macabre, Machen unfurls this tale of a young girl cursed by her supernatural parentage. This new, exclusive edition from Creation Press includes a set of complementary "automatic" drawings by Machen's contemporary and fellow mystic, **Austin Osman Spare**, and a brand new introductory essay on Machen and his works by Iain Smith of the Arthur Machen Society, as well as Machen's own illuminating introduction from the 1916 edition.
*"What can I say about a writer whose influence has been acknowledged by H.P. Lovecraft, Peter Straub, and Clive Barker? Perhaps that he managed to communicate a sense of the inexpressibly and awesomely supernatural with more power than he ever knew."* — **RAMSEY CAMPBELL**
*"Of creators of cosmic fear raised to its most artistic pitch, few can hope to equal Arthur Machen"* — **H. P. LOVECRAFT**
**£7.95**

**"SALOME"**　Oscar Wilde　　　　　*Creation Classics VI*
Written — and banned — in 1892, **Salome** is Oscar Wilde's ultimate, most *outré* statement of Decadence. Composed in French, this bizarre Biblical psychodrama was eventually translated from the original French by his friend Lord Alfred Douglas.
Blasphemous, erotic-charged, masturbatory, oneiric, hypnotic: this concentric tale of lust, sexual jealousy and violent murder is above all a savage attack on the hypocritical misogyny of Christianity.
This brand new edition from Creation Press includes original illustrations drafted by **Aubrey Beardsley** for the English translation, and also features an archaic translation of The Book of Revelation (whence Wilde drew much of the apocalytic imagery in **Salome**): the book of Armagideon and the Beast 666.
**£7.95**

# THE CREATION PUBLISHING GROUP
83, Clerkenwell Road, London EC1. Tel/Fax: 071 430 9878
*Representation:*
DIRECTION
Suite 1, Royal Star Arcade, High Street, Maidstone, Kent ME14 1JL.
Tel: 0622 764555　Fax: 0622 763197
*Distribution:*
COMBINED BOOK SERVICES
406 Vale Road, Tonbridge, Kent TN9 1XR.
Tel: 0732 357755　Fax: 0732 770219